HIDDEN IN THE HORIZON

THE BIGGEST IMPACT CAN COME FROM THE SMALLEST SMILE

J.L. Schaffer

First edition February 2026
Published by Get It Write Publishing & Editing

Printed in the United States of America
ISBN: 979-8-9993421-5-7

ACKNOWLEDGMENTS

I want to begin by expressing my heartfelt gratitude to everyone who read my debut novel, *Caught in the Horizon*. Your support and encouragement meant so much to me as I embarked on this writing journey.

I am deeply thankful for my friends and family. Their unwavering support throughout the process of writing both books has been invaluable. Their belief in me has helped carry me through the challenges and joys of storytelling.

My beautiful wife, Kaylynn, deserves special recognition. Along with our children—Jordan, Jake, Josh, and Kadi—and our additional son, Owl, they have all been a source of love and motivation. I am grateful to my mother, Diane, and my Aunt Sandi for their constant encouragement. My grandson, Daxton, brings joy to my life and inspires me to face any difficulties that come my way. Papa loves you, little man.

I also wish to acknowledge my colleagues and the students on my bus #8. Their honest opinions and thoughtful input have helped shape my adventure and propelled it forward. Their feedback—always candid—has been essential in my progress.

I am grateful for my new friend and fellow author, Jamie S. Farrington (*Hidden Among The Leaves*). Jamie listened to my concerns and the growing pains that come with writing books. It has been incredibly helpful to discuss these challenges with someone who truly understands the dilemmas writers face.

My sincere thanks go to Get It Write Publishing for handling my second book with professionalism and making the process feel smooth and easy.

A Personal Reflection

In this unpredictable world, hardships and sadness often come unexpectedly. The loss of friends and family members can be sudden, and whether the reasons are clear or not, such moments are life-altering. We can never truly know what others are thinking or how alone someone may feel. Sometimes, a simple smile, a wave, or asking about someone's day might make a significant difference in their lives. Kindness costs nothing; a small gesture like opening a door or spending a few minutes talking to an old friend can mean the world to someone.

I have personally experienced the pain of losing friends and family to suicide, often without seeing any warning signs. Some seemed to have everything—a good job, a loving family, and deep affection for their loved ones and pets. Yet, it is impossible to know what someone is truly going through. Cherish your loved ones, hug them as often as you can, and keep a smile on your face. That embrace might be the last—or it might lead to many more wonderful moments together.

Thanks for reading my books, I hope you enjoy them.

J.L Schaffer

(Fishhooks Forever)

TABLE OF CONTENTS

Chapter 1

"You'll never feel at home, when you're all alone." –Hunter

Hunter walks through the woods, stone-faced. Not one emotion can be seen. His body is numb to its surroundings, yet he continues to move forward toward Fat Jack's cave. Knowing the cave is less than a mile away, Hunter notices an old, weathered stump, so he decides to sit for a moment and wait for his emotions to catch up with him. Exhausted, he lowers his head toward the ground and leans his pool stick beside the stump. It doesn't take long before the tears begin to follow each other down Hunter's face. Hunter finds himself alone once more. He thinks, *Am I that bad of a person? Why am I destined to be alone?*

After sitting in silence for what seems to him like hours, Hunter hears the snapping of a stick, drawing his attention. He grabs his pool stick and yells, "Who's there? I suggest you show yourself, or I'll make you a memory!"

A smaller-looking Shadow steps out from behind a thornbush. Hunter can tell the Shadow is frightened and not much of a threat, as it timidly steps out in front of him.

"Are you alone?" Hunter asks cautiously.

The Shadow nods yes, remaining silent.

Hunter points his stick at the scared Shadow and shouts, "Tell me why I shouldn't just release you right where you're standing!"

The Shadow timidly remarks, "Sir, I mean you no harm. I mean *nobody* any harm. As you see, I do not carry a weapon, nor do I want to. Believe it or not, not all Shadows want to be evil."

Hunter sighs. "Really? Because I ain't ever met a good one. The only good Shadow I know of is a released one!"

The now-confused Shadow changes the subject. "Why are you

sitting here alone, crying? You won the war; you're on the winning side. You should be celebrating with the kings."

"It sure doesn't feel like I'm a winner. Haven't you ever heard that nobody wins in war? Yeah, my prize for winning was to never see my sister, best friends, or happiness ever again. Yep, that makes me a big winner."

The Shadow sits on the ground, pondering Hunter's sarcasm. "I'm sorry. I guess I've lost the ability to have feelings. Once I became a Shadow, I lost every memory I had. We became clean slates. Please continue. Tell me about your loss. This way, maybe I can share some of your pain, so you will not have to carry it alone."

Hunter stares at the Shadow, still not believing the words coming out of its mouth. He's so angry he could spit. "You took my sister, my best friend, and my Bug! You took Dillo and Cam. You took a sweet, innocent little girl's leg. The only thing Colt wanted to do was run, and you took that from her!"

The Shadow begins to slowly slide backwards as Hunter continues. "Our whole lives, we were bullied, put down, made fun of, threatened, and intimidated. Our world made us give up. We wanted to leave it behind us. Why couldn't you just leave us alone? What did we ever do to you? We fought demons in our world, and now we have to fight them in *this* world. Why, no matter where we go, does hate have to follow us?" Hunter turns his stick onto himself, placing his chin on the end of it.

The Shadow stands and tries to calm the situation down. "You won! Now that you've won, you can change the Horizon and make it a nice place for everyone. Sir, please don't do this. Your light is the last thing you have left. You can't do this to your friends again. You do this, and your sister and best friends gave their lights up for nothing."

Hunter wipes the tears from his face with one hand, as the other still holds the stick to his chin. His hand begins to shake, so he puts the stick down. Then, as though none of that happened, Hunter begins to walk away.

Scared and confused, the Shadow asks, "Where are you going?"

Hunter doesn't turn around; he simply says, "Home."

The surprised Shadow raises his voice. "You're just going to walk away? You're not going to release me? I guess there are still some good guys in the Horizon."

Hunter stops and turns around. "With what I've done here and what you made me do here, trust me, I am definitely not a good guy. Now it's my turn to be the bad guy."

Hunter draws his stick as the Shadow's eyes widen. Before another word is said, Hunter releases the Shadow and then continues down his path. He looks toward the sky. "Guys, I think it's time to introduce myself to this Hangman. Maybe if I ask nicely, he'll just hand over Spin Doll." He smiles. "If not, I'll make him a memory. This one's for you, Kannon."

Chapter 2

"You never know what to expect behind a closed door." –Hunter

Approaching Fat Jack's cave, Hunter first notices the front door has been left open. He whispers to the emptiness, "You guys know this is a trap. If anything moves, it won't anymore."

He circles around, trying to get a better look inside. Still not seeing any movement, Hunter yells through the door. "Hey, if anyone's in there, show yourself! Don't make us come in, guns blaring."

Nobody answers, and he still doesn't see any movement. Moving closer toward the gently swinging door, Hunter yells again. "Mr. Hangman, come on out! You're our next contestant. There are a couple guys out here who would like to speak with you. You might have heard of them. One's named Smith, and the other's name is Wesson."

Still, not a sound comes from the door, which frustrates Hunter. "I'm going to toss a rock in the door. That should draw them out." He fires a rock into the cave and hears something break inside. With no response, Hunter walks up to the door. Still not seeing any movement, despite being able to see much more inside, Hunter looks back and whispers, "Well, guys, I guess it's like when a bitch has you by the balls. You're going where she wants you to go, whether you like it or not." He laughs out loud, then walks in like he owns the place.

There really isn't much inside—a bathroom, a kitchen, and a small living area with a recliner facing twenty doors. Each door has its own unique look. None of them have names on them, which makes it impossible to tell whose door belongs to whom. Hunter wonders how Jack knows who owns each. Two doors have musical notes on them. Is it Spin Doll's because of her music box, or is it his because he is— *was*—a singer?

Then he notices another has a rope—or is it a whip? —etched on it, which could be Spin Doll's or Lakin's.

Hunter realizes he is overthinking too much, so he just *eenie, meanie, miny, moes it.* When he finishes, he finds himself standing in front of a yellow door with a black rainbow on it. Hunter pulls out the only key and holds it up, waiting for the door to respond. Nothing happens, which makes Hunter wonder if the key even works at all. He tries touching different spots on the door, but still nothing happens. There aren't any keyholes, and the key itself is round, like a small Frisbee.

Frustrated and about to give up, Hunter looks to the sky. "Do you guys have any ideas?"

Then, by accident, he grazes the doorknob with the key, and the door pops open. Looking inside, he sees a wooded area. Hunter's first thought is that it must be where Kannon is from, which means he has to get to Kannon before he pulls that trigger.

After entering, it doesn't take him long to find an old, paved road that looks like it hasn't been maintained in quite some time, and he begins to run down it. He chooses to go right first (video game code of conduct). It isn't long before the road leads to a clearing. He is sure this is where Kannon was supposed to meet Dayne. Off in the distance, he notices an outline of a person. The closer he gets, the more familiar the person looks.

He yells, "Hey, are you alright?"

The person looks toward him but doesn't answer. As he moves closer, Hunter yells again. "Hey, I'm talking to you. Are you okay?"

Once again, the person doesn't answer. It's as if he is in his own little world and can't hear him.

Now running toward the figure, Hunter yells with every ounce of air in his body, "Stop! Hey, guy, you need to put that down. Please put that down. Spin Doll needs you."

The figure continues as if he has not heard Hunter. With one last attempt, Hunter begs, "Please, don't do what you're thinking. This world needs you more than you know. *I* need you more than you know."

The man stops and looks at Hunter. "*You* need me? Why do you need *me?*"

"I need you to help me save Spin Doll, and because you're my best friend."

"Sorry, never heard of a Spin Doll. How can we be best friends? I've never even seen you before."

"Listen, we *are* best friends, and I really do need your help. So please come down and talk to me."

"If you are my best friend, then what's my name? Why am I up here?"

Hunter smiles. "You're my best friend, and your name is Bug. You're up here because today is your graduation day, and you thought you'd lost everything. Oh, and that bat you're holding—its name is Babe. But not after Babe Ruth."

Bug looks down from the top of the bridge and smiles. "How'd you know it's my graduation day? Plus, I didn't name this bat; I just found it lying on the ground. Who names a bat?"

"I know because I'm your best friend. You named that bat "Babe" after the best little league baseball player you've ever met: Babe Schmit."

Bug is shocked, wondering how Hunter knows all this about him. It's stuff that Bug has never mentioned to anyone.

Stepping closer, Bug says, "Mister, I don't know how you know all of that, but this world doesn't want me. As for this bat, you can have it." He throws the bat down at Hunter's feet.

Hunter immediately begins to climb the bridge.

Bug yells, "What—are you crazy? You don't want to come up here."

Hunter continues to climb. "Well, if you're jumping, then I'm jumping. I'm not letting my friend go out alone." Soon, Hunter is standing beside Bug, and they both stare at the ground below.

"Man, why are you doing this? This is *my* problem, not yours."

Hunter continues looking at the ground below them. "Your problem has now become my problem. If I can't count on your help, then we might as well jump."

"Mister, I'm not who you think I am. I'm a nobody. Trust me, I can't help you. Shit, I can't help myself. Look where I am and what I'm about to do. Please get down. I don't want to be the cause of two lives."

"So, are you jumping first, or am I? Because the only way I'm getting down is the method you choose for us."

Realizing Hunter isn't going to leave, Bug decides to climb back down (only until Hunter is down safely), but Hunter has already caught on to Bug's plan. "You first. I'll follow you down."

Bug reluctantly leads the way down until they are safely on the ground. Hunter remains between Bug and the bridge, explaining his reason for being there. "I met you in the Horizon, after you took your selfish leap. We became friends and battle buddies, all for the sake of the Horizon. We saved the kings, and in the process, you fell in love with a girl named Spin Doll."

Bug scoffs. "This must be another one of my stupid dreams."

"No, it's very much real. This girl, Spin Doll, loved you as well. In the battle for the kingdom, this evil man named Jim and his creature dragged Spin Doll back into this world. I was sent to rescue her, and I need your help."

"If she was my girlfriend and we were best friends, why didn't I come back with you?"

Hunter really doesn't want to tell Bug he has been released, so he answers, "They couldn't afford to let us all go. Plus, you were more valuable back in the Horizon. Also, we couldn't have two of you occupying one place. Now, are you going to help me, or am I heading back up to the bridge?"

Bug thinks for a minute. "I'll help you find this Spin Doll. But after you do, you leave me be."

Hunter agrees, and they head back toward town.

Chapter 3

"To have a child so unique that its gender is seen differently through the eyes of who processes it makes a parent just as proud as confused." –Spin Doll

Jim walks ahead as Hangman continues to drag Spin Doll behind him. Suddenly, he stops. "Stupid! Pick her up and carry her on your shoulder. That way we can walk faster."

The Hangman does as he is told and tosses Spin Doll over his shoulder. Walking through what looks like an abandoned city, Jim looks down every alleyway they pass.

Frustrated, Jim says, We'll never find that damn child at this rate. Set her down over there on that stoop while I think this out." He points to an abandoned building's steps.

The Hangman drops Spin Doll on the staircase with a thud. Spin Doll gasps for air as the sudden fall knocks the wind out of her. She rolls over and sits up with a smile on her face. This annoys Jim.

"What are you laughing about? Have you lost your friggin' mind? You know, once we find that little boy, we no longer need you."

Spin Doll, still smiling, replies, "Now that we've returned home, I get to kill you twice. I get to make you a memory."

Jim rushes up and grabs Spin Doll, angrily yelling, "I'll end you where you sit, bitch! Tell me where that little brat is, and we won't make you suffer."

Spin Doll pulls her head back away from Jim's hand, then counters, "I wonder if you'll scream as much as your fat brother did when I ended him."

Jim is losing his patience and getting nowhere. "I'll be right back! You keep an eye on our prisoner." Then he storms off, leaving Spin Doll alone with Hangman.

The Hangman stands next to Spin Doll, never saying a word. Spin Doll looks toward Hangman, but not for too long. He reaches over and twists her head, forcing her to look forward. Even though she tries not to look scared, she is terrified of this purely evil creature.

After a bit of silence, Spin Doll says, "Mr. Hangman, sir, I need to go to the bathroom." When he doesn't answer, she speaks boldly again. "At least get me a drink. I think I'm dehydrated." She holds up her hands to show how shaky they are.

Still, Hangman doesn't acknowledge her. Spin Doll sits quietly, wondering where child is.

The two remain silent for quite some time. Eventually, Jim returns holding a little boy's jacket. He holds it up in front of Spin Doll. "Does this look familiar?"

Spin Doll's eyes widen. "No, sorry, never seen that before."

Her eyes tell another story to Jim, though. He smiles as he waves the jacket in front of Spin Doll. "Looks like a little boy's or girl's jacket. I'd say he or she must be like two or three years old. Oh, and look, it has a little bumblebee on it." Jim knows Spin Doll's child's name is Bee.

Spin Doll continues to act as if she doesn't know who the owner of the jacket is.

Jim hands the jacket to Hangman, who rips it in half, destroying it. "So, rumor has it you left your child with an old street dog named Diesel." Spin Doll doesn't answer, still playing dumb, and Jim starts to lose his cool. "Let me get this right. You left your helpless two-year-old child named Bee with a hungry stray dog that nobody, willingly, will approach." He leans closer, not waiting for a response, and whispers, "Nice of you to leave him lunch. I'm sure by now he's already eaten' 'em. Poor little Bee. Or should we just call him dog food? What kind of mother are you? I mean, really, you left him here to be dog food."

Many thoughts run through Spin Doll's head, but she remains silent. Before their one-sided discussion can continue, they are approached by three rough-looking men.

Jim yells, "Leave us be. Now is not the time!"

The biggest of the three men says, "Well, well, well, what do we have here—a lady, an old man, and a mute. How about it goes like this: you give us everything you have, and we'll let one of you live." One of the other two men blows a kiss toward Spin Doll.

Jim smiles as he takes a seat next to Spin Doll on the stoop. "Gentlemen—and I use that term loosely—the way I see it, you three have definitely not thought this over. I'll tell you what; you tell us where we might be able to find a little child named Bee. Maybe, just maybe, my friend here will leave one of you alive."

The bigger man chuckles. "Get a load of the balls on this one."

Then the third man pulls out a knife. "Are you *loco,* old man? At first, we felt sorry for you, so we were going to let you be the one to live. Now I'm hoping you at least put up a fight before we cut you in half."

Jim whispers to Spin Doll, "Watch this. It's going to be good."

The man with the knife swings at Hangman. The Hangman intercepts the knife as he rips the man's arm off and stabs him in the neck with his own knife. The bigger man points to the other man to attack Hangman. Before the charging man can do anything, Hangman twists the man's head in a complete 360, ripping it from his body and tossing it to the ground. The bigger man tries to run but is caught before he can take a step. The man screams in pain as he dangles by his hair. With Hangman holding him in the air by his hair, Jim approaches. The man begs Jim to make Hangman release him.

Jim, relishing his power, says, "Now, before all of this, I simply asked you if you knew of a little child's whereabouts. No, you had to be a tough guy. Now look at where that's gotten you. Because I'm such a nice guy, I'm going to give you another chance to answer that question."

The man dangling in pain quickly begs, "I'll tell you anything; just please put me down."

Jim stands in front of the man with his hands behind his back as he nods for Hangman to lower the man to the ground. Once the man's feet hit the ground, he quickly reaches up to feel the top of his head. With his hands covered in blood, he answers, "The little boy is in the five-story building on Layman Ave. He's on floor three—I think apartment twenty-one. Now, please let me go. You said you would let one of us live. You remember that, right?"

Jim pats the little man on the chest. "You sure are right; I truly did say that. How about right this minute we both agree that I am a liar?"

Before the man can respond, Hangman crushes his head between his hands. Jim turns to look at Spin Doll, noticing that she is gone, as the man's lifeless body falls to the ground beside his friends.

Jim lowers his voice and orders, "Find her and bring me back the child. Also, we only need the child alive, so dispose of Spin Doll however you see fit."

The Hangman walks off down the street without saying a word. Once out of sight, Jim mumbles, "Once I have the child, your services will no longer be needed as well."

Chapter 4

"Never make a deal with the devil, no matter how bleak the situation." –Spin Doll

Without being seen, Spin Doll quietly hops off the stoop and climbs through a broken window, which takes her to the building's basement. Finding it hard to navigate her way through the abandoned basement by the light of a few small windows, Spin Doll makes it to the stairway, taking each step slowly. A few of the steps are broken or missing completely. But, nonetheless, she makes it to the first floor. Quickly stepping from one doorway to the next, she is at the back door in no time. The big metal back door is rusty and hard to push open. Trying to keep the door's creaking noise to a minimum, she pushes it just enough to slide through. Spin Doll slips out the door and into an even worse alleyway and hides behind an overflowing dumpster, watching and waiting for a chance to make a run for it. She peers around the disgusting dumpster to see if she is alone in the alleyway, which is littered with garbage. She slowly moves from the dumpster to the other side of the alley. Spin Doll cannot believe how bad her world has gotten. This used to be such an up-and-coming city. Now it is filled with lowlifes and crime. Finally, she makes it to the end of the alley, where she can better see her dilapidated city.

Pinned against the alleyway wall, Spin Doll searches for her next move. Suddenly, she hears footsteps coming toward her. She very slightly looks around the corner of the building, her eyes widening when she sees Hangman walking in her direction. Knowing she doesn't have the time to make it back to the dumpster, she jumps behind a smaller pile of garbage bags. As silently as possible, she lies in the filthy street behind the bags, praying Hangman can't see her. She can hear the footsteps coming closer. The footsteps stop as a bead of sweat rolls down Spin Doll's forehead. She dares not look up and give herself away. A sound comes from the other end of the alley wall, prompting Hangman to enter the alley. Spin Doll remains quiet as Hangman stops in front of the garbage bags that hide her. He is close enough to her that she can see his shadow and hear his heavy breathing. They both remain silent as she refuses to move, and he stands looking down the alley. Thinking this might be her end, she refuses to move. From the dumpster, a stray cat jumps, landing on an unsuspecting rat. The rat squeals in pain as the cat destroys it. The Hangman begins to laugh, but it is a weird sound. It's as if he is laughing but doesn't know how to do so. He stands and watches till the rat has no life left. Then he turns and leaves the alley, heading back to his next target.

Spin Doll rolls to her back and takes a deep breath, wiping tears from her eyes, knowing she can't defeat Hangman. After a few minutes, she recovers her composure and stands up.

Before she can take a step, a voice can be heard from the street into the alley.

"Well, that was a pretty close one, wasn't it?" Jim says as he rounds the corner.

Spin Doll doesn't know whether to run or attack the old man. She draws her fans and confronts him. "Can't you leave me alone? You lost the Horizon; now go torment someone else. I think I've had my share."

Jim smiles. "Now, now, I wouldn't be too loud. You wouldn't want Hangman to hear you. I can make this really simple. You give me Baby Bee, and I'll make the mean Hangman go away for good."

Spin Doll lowers her voice as she informs Jim, "I'll never give you Baby Bee! You'll have to release me first."

Jim steps closer and kicks an old can out of his way. "Don't worry. I'm sure your release will come soon enough. But I need that baby! You see, with that little bee—or should I say, *storyteller*—I can still be the ruler of the Horizon."

"You sick bastard!" Spin Doll shouts. "I'll never let you have my baby!"

"Enough! We both know he's not your actual baby. You know, in order to *have* a baby, you must first have relations. So, tell me, where's the storyteller?"

Spin Doll, still refusing to give up Bee's whereabouts, states, "Go to hell, old man! You'll never find him."

"I've been to hell; it's not as bad of a place as you'd think. You know, another fun fact: that's where I met Hangman. Us bad guys have a meeting there once a month." Then he impatiently states, "Now, for the final time… Where's the little storyteller, Bee?"

Spin Doll won't answer. She simply shakes her head.

Jim, frustrated and at the end of his rope, begins to walk toward Spin Doll. Spin Doll, not backing down, walks toward Jim. But before they reach each other, Spin Doll hears a dull thud. Jim falls to the ground face-first, knocked out, as a decent-sized rock rolls along the ground. There, standing behind the out-cold Jim, is a young girl about twelve years old. Spin Doll's face grows into a large smile as she squeals, "Jax! Am I glad to see you!"

The young girl runs up to Spin Doll and gives her a big hug. "You came back! I knew you would."

Spin Doll hugs her as well. "Look how big you've gotten. Where's Bee? We need to get the baby now."

Jax smiles. "I'm the same size, and Diesel is watching him. They're only a few blocks away. I had to move him because this area was getting way worse than it had been."

Spin Doll wastes no time. She informs Jax of the situation, and they head off to Bee's hidden location.

A faking Jim smiles upon hearing this without opening his eyes.

Chapter 5

"Some things you can't believe unless you witness it." –Dak

Dak and Hoss scour the kingdom's land, dispensing any and all Shadows they come across. They clear the barn, factory, Dayne's house, and where the witch's house once stood. They soon make it to their old campsite on the high hill. Hoss stops at Dillo's field to reminisce and bury the remaining shell pieces. Once finished, Dak explains to Hoss about the little farm that Dillo visited often and where they had gotten the eggs from. Hoss wants to thank them personally, so Dak leads the way.

As they approach the farm, they see that the fields are extremely high and not at all maintained. Animals wander, looking for food.

Dak is disappointed. "This farm was immaculate when we were last here."

"Well, it's not now, bub," Hoss blurts.

They search the farm and find the old farmer rocking in a chair on the porch, staring out into nowhere.

As they tentatively approach the man, Dak says, "Sir, are you alright? What happened to the farm?"

The old man continues rocking, and without looking at the men, he replies, "My wife couldn't take the news of losing Dillo. Since we never had kids of our own in either world, he soon became her little boy. Once she passed, I had nothing to work for. I figured I've worked long and hard enough. If I couldn't earn my star with all the blood, sweat, and tears I've put into the land, then I'd just stop and sit here and rock." He pauses, still staring out into nowhere. "You know what, boy? In our last world, we worked hard and lived right. We helped neighbors in times of need and prayed to a higher power. We came here thinking we could rest and enjoy ourselves, maybe even dance in the rain. But, no, we were handed another plot of land and a little house. We did what we knew how to do—work. Now, my wife is gone; I have no dance partner, and I'm tired. So, I'm done. I'm going to sit here and rock."

Dak doesn't know how to answer the old man's words, but Hoss steps in. "Sir, I thank you. Thank you for putting food on people's tables. I thank you for working a job most won't do from morning to night. I thank your hard-working, cracked hands and your beautiful wife, who was by your side through all your hardships and smiles. Our last world, as well as this world, truly doesn't recognize what you've done for them. I, being a soldier, understand how easily people forget the sacrifices we make. For your hard work and sacrifices, I would truly like to thank you and your wife." Hoss turns and walks away as the old man continues to rock.

Dak now feels awful for both the farmer and Hoss, and he stands there, speechless for a moment before waving to the farmer and turning to leave.

The farmer speaks up again. "I appreciated your friend's words, and please tell him I thank him as well."

Dak nods and continues walking when he hears the farmer add, "Angel. I ain't no angel. I'm just a tired old dirt farmer."

When Dak catches up with Hoss, Hoss seems a little different, as if speaking with the old farmer has tired him out as well. They walk for a bit in silence.

Eventually, Hoss says, "I think that old farmer and I have a lot in common. I'm tired too. I thought leaving my world, I'd finally have peace. But no, even here, there is fighting, hating, evil, and corruption. Is that all we have? Are we all just bad? I mean, sure, we think we're on the good side, but are we? What if we're not, and we just destroyed the good side again?"

"Of course we're on the good side."

Hoss shakes his head. "Oh yeah—if we're on the good side, then why'd that old farmer and his wife have to go through all the struggles and pain again? What could they have possibly done wrong in their previous lives to not become stars? What the hell more do I have to do to be a star?"

Dak doesn't know the answer to that, but Hoss continues. "I took my own life to escape the pain and thoughts I had. I just wanted peace. I ended up here only to take more lives and relive my pain." Hoss begins to slow down and eventually stops, plopping down on the ground.

"What are you doing? We can make it back to the kingdom by nightfall if we don't stop."

Hoss takes a deep breath. "Yeah, buddy, I think I'm done. I'm done walking; I'm done fighting; I'm just done. You go and save the kingdom, the leader of the angels. That's what you were to become. I, myself, am going to go and sit in the field and talk to my good friend, Dillo. I guess this is where we part, my friend."

Dak anxiously pleads, "No, no, please. You have to come back with me. We still have a lot to do to save the kingdom."

Hoss pats Dak on the shoulder. "You got this, boy. I'm just a tired old soldier who needs to rest."

"What about Dayne, Hunter, or me? We need you now more than ever."

Hoss smiles. "No, you don't; you're all good now. Who *does* need me is the rest of our friends. Colt, Cam, Bug, and Kannon are a team, you know. Besides, Dillo needs me more than you all. Someone needs to protect him from the geese and goats."

Dak can't believe what Hoss is saying. Is he really going to lose another friend? Hoss gives Dak a hug and sends him off on his way to the kingdom. Dak stumbles forward, not believing he is leaving his friend for good. Hoss, in return, stands and walks in the direction of Dillo's shell. Dak really can't believe what he is told, so he follows Hoss without being seen. He watches as Hoss walks to Dillo's final resting place and sits beside him. He isn't close enough to hear what Hoss is saying, but he can see him moving his hands and speaking to the sky.

Dak really wishes he could hear, so he moves in closer. Once he is within earshot, he hears Hoss say, "Well, Dillo, my old friend, I think it's time to give up. With your help, we won the battle. I think the war is far from over. But this soldier is done fighting."

Dak watches as Hoss pulls a Starletta from his pocket and cracks it open. He quickly finishes it and lies back on the grass. From the other side of the field, Dak notices a small group of Shadows forming. There must be about seven of them. Dak figures Hoss knows they are there and will dispose of them quickly. The Shadows charge as Hoss just lies there. Dak wants to yell but can't. He watches the Shadows hack and slash without Hoss putting up a fight. After what seems like a lifetime, Dak watches as Hoss's light floats up from his body as the Shadows dance and cheer. Dak feels differently about watching his friend give up like that. The same thought keeps racing through his head: *How can you just give up like that?*

Chapter 6

"Sometimes seeing old faces is just what you need." –Spin Doll

When Jim comes to his senses, he sits up with an even worse attitude. He stands up while rubbing the back of his head. As he rubs, he feels a large bump on the back of his head, which is sore to the touch, and he grimaces each time. Jim angrily kicks some trash that lies strewn across the alley as he walks out into the street. Looking up and down the street, he sees no one. With his temper ready to explode, he screams, "Spin Doll! You're finished. When I get my hands on you, I'll make sure Baby Bee will never know your name. Whoever hit me from behind, your time is numbered as well."

Jim slowly walks down the street, looking in every window and alleyway, he passes. He mumbles, "First, I have a brain-dead imbecile out looking for a baby in this rundown city. Why can't anything be easy?"

While talking to himself, two young lowlifes approach him. The smaller man demands, "Hey, old timer, can't you hear? My friend here wants your money and your shoes. Maybe I'll have to beat them off you."

Jim looks disgusted. "Young man, I have neither the time nor the patience to deal with you at the moment. So please step aside."

The two lowlifes look at each other in disbelief at what Jim has just said. The big one punches his fist into his hand. "I like it when they won't give it up. It makes me all tingly inside knowing I get to hurt somebody."

"Well, if you want to beat someone up, beat up your friend here. Shit, he looks like he's been beaten before."

The smaller one yells, "You want some of me, old man? Well, it looks like I'm a genie, because I'm about to grant your wish."

He swings at Jim, but Jim steps aside and grabs each side of the man's head and twists it in a complete one-eighty. The smaller man now drops to his knees, lifeless. The big man's eyes widen as he turns to run. But he's just as unlucky as his small friend, due to the fact that Hangman is standing behind him. The big man stands no chance, as his arms are both torn from his body. With blood shooting from both sides, he collapses near his friend.

Jim looks at Hangman. "What are you doing back here already?"

In a low, crackly voice, Hangman answers while holding out the other man's hand toward Jim. "I thought you might need a hand."

Jim rolls his eyes. "Three days I've been with you. This is the first thing you say to me. Hell, I didn't think you could speak, let alone be a comedian."

The Hangman stares at Jim with no response. Jim shakes his head as he begins to walk away, mumbling, "Every single day I have to deal with dumb. Why should today be any different?"

The Hangman turns to follow him.

* * *

Seven blocks away, Jax leads Spin Doll through a maze of rooms and traps to get to Bee. Eventually, they come to a thick wooden door. Jax places his ear to the door, then knocks three times. Nothing happens as Spin Doll patiently waits. Then Jax knocks four more times, and they can now hear movement from the other side of the door like something large is being pushed around. Suddenly, they hear the sound of locks unlocking. Jax backs away from the door as Spin Doll pulls her fans out.

The door slowly opens, revealing the largest dog Spin Doll has ever seen. Jax lunges forward and bear hugs the dog while yelling, "Diesel, look who's home! It's Cali."

Even with Jax wrapped around the large dog, Diesel pounces on Spin Doll, pinning her to the floor. Spin Doll tries to get up before she drowns in dog saliva. She can't believe the size of Diesel. When she left, Diesel was just a puppy.

Spin Doll asks Jax, "What have you been feeding him?"

Jax chuckles. "You know, the normal food—bones and small cars. What size did you think a Great Dane/Mastiff mix pup would be?"

Once they get Diesel calmed down, they entered the room. Lying on a small dog bed in the middle of the room is little Baby Bee, fast asleep. Even though Spin Doll can't wait to hold him, she lets little Bee sleep.

Chapter 7

"Truthful words hit the hardest." –Dayne

With the four kings back in power and the threat of the Shadows almost eliminated, the kings take to their thrones and begin filling the sky with stars. Dayne watches at first as the lights come in from the other kings. Paragon invites her over to watch and learn. Dayne stands beside him as the first light approaches.

"Ahh, Clyde, my friend, how have you been? It's been a long time. How has your time in the Horizon treated you?"

The light answers, "My king, I've been very good. As you remember, I was about to be a star before the Jokers turned us all into Shadows. My king, it was such an awful experience. I truly understand if I'm not ready to be a star."

Paragon nods. "Clyde, my son, today is the day you will join the night sky and become a star."

With no other words spoken, the light orb becomes incredibly bright. A little star cleaner flies up into the sky and places the new star in its forever spot. The star shines so brightly it's hard to look at.

Paragon explains, "When the orb is in front of you, you'll be able to see them in their earthly form. Also, their names will appear. You will pass judgment on them by granting them their star or by refusing for the time being and making them be angels in the Horizon until they earn their light."

"What about those who were already stars?"

"Those you send up without judgment. You can tell they were formerly stars by the gold shimmer in their eyes."

Furrow interjects. "I would suggest you begin. The line at your throne has grown quite large."

Dayne, without hesitation, sits on her throne. The very first orb she deals with is a young girl in her late teens. Softly, Dayne says, "My child… I mean, Grace. What have you to say in regard to becoming a star?"

Grace replies, "My king, even though I am young, I have done only good and have been told I have an old soul."

Dayne chuckles by accident, remembering her first meeting with Cam. That was exactly what he said.

"What makes a good person?" Dayne questions.

Grace thinks for a minute. "Love, compassion, and caring, I suppose."

Dayne's body warms, as if telling her Grace is good. She nods. "I can see you have a sleeve tattoo. What does it mean?"

Grace pulls her sleeve up to reveal the whole tattoo. "This is my gram. She kept our whole family on the straight and narrow. If it weren't for her love, our family wouldn't be the people we are. The images around her picture are what we loved and shared together. These roses are because we tended to a flower bed together. This fox is from when I found a lost baby fox. Gram and I nursed it to good health, then returned it to the woods. This big plate of pasta is for the Sunday family dinners she made the whole family attend."

As Grace explains this with a smile, Dayne feels more goodness in her heart. She stops Grace and grants her star form. "Any last words before you take your place in the sky?"

A smiling Grace yells, "Gram, your baby girl is coming to see you!"

Mim carries Grace up to the sky, and Dayne feels more happiness than she ever has before. She gestures for the next in line. A middle-aged man approaches and says his name is Gene. Dayne doesn't receive the same feeling she had with Grace and questions, "What have you to say in regard to becoming a star?"

Gene quickly replies, "I've been mostly good. But does it matter? We will all become stars either way."

Dayne is a little stunned by Gene's reply. She notices a tattoo on him as well. "I see you have a tattoo. What is the meaning of the 'Death to a Coward' design?"

Gene looks at his arm. "Oh, this stupid thing. That's from kids being kids. I got it on a dare. It's no biggie. Everyone's done stupid things in their life."

Dayne has a bad feeling about this one. Does she send him up to the sky not to hurt his feelings? Confused, Dayne waves to Truncheon to try to get his attention. When he approaches, she whispers, "What do I do if I feel they shouldn't be a star at this moment?"

Truncheon places his hand on Dayne's shoulder. "You are a king. You do not have to explain your decisions. They must accept what you choose. If they are not star quality, then you don't grant it. Be as truthful as you can. They will understand."

Dayne turns to Gene. "You will not become a star today. My decision is final."

Though Gene is stunned, he doesn't argue, just thanks her for her time and leaves with new work orders. Dayne feels awful about that decision.

Truncheon pats her shoulder. "You'll make an excellent king." Then he leaves for his throne and waiting orbs.

Dayne thinks, *how could this get any worse?* When she turns, she gasps. Standing in front of her is Kannon. Dayne remains frozen while Kannon watches her. Not knowing if he can recognize her, Dayne says, "Kannon, to become a star, you must have reason and ideas for what a star must be."

"I would not want to be a star," Kanon shockingly responds.

Surprised, Dayne inquires, "Why would you not want to be a star? Everyone wants to be a star."

"My beautiful wife and son are here in the Horizon. I must find them and protect them," he truthfully explains.

That's when it hits Dayne: Kannon doesn't recognize her. *How does he not know it's me? I'm standing in front of him.*

"What does your wife look like, if I may ask?" she inquires.

Kannon replies without hesitation. "Why, she's the most beautiful sight your eyes would ever have the pleasure to gaze on, with her red flowing hair and bright, twinkling eyes. To see her smile makes you smile. With a room full of people, she'd be the only one you'd notice. To own her heart is to own everything. I must walk beside her, because if I walk behind her, she takes my breath away, leaving me gasping for air. No, she's the one. *Perfect* became a word after seeing her. So, you see, I must decline, for my star in the Horizon is here on this ground."

Hearing this makes Dayne realize the true power of love. Kannon would give up his chance for eternal happiness just to love her for another day. The emotions hit Dayne so hard that she stands and walks away, leaving Kannon with no judgment.

Furrow sees her head to the tower, so he leaves his throne to check on her. He finds her sitting in the stairwell with tear-filled eyes. Furrow hugs Dayne, not knowing why the tears are there. Dayne begins rocking back and forth as she explains. "I cannot do this. I'm not the right choice to be king. Please pick another. I don't want it."

Furrow agrees. "I did not want this as well, but who can we trust with such a job? Many of my friends and family have come in front of me. Trust me, it never gets easier."

"I seriously can't do it. The pain of seeing my husband and him not knowing me—we were so in love. How can I send him up there knowing I may never see him again?"

"He will never lose his love for you, and this is true. But someday you will join him because it was meant to be." Furrow stands up. "You were chosen; now go fulfill your purpose."

Dayne doesn't respond as Furrow returns to his throne. She finally stands and exits the back door of the tower and doesn't stop till she's standing at the edge of the kingdom. For a while, Dayne looks back at the wondrous kingdom.

Chapter 8

"It's all fun and games until you're losing." –Bug

Heading into town, Hunter asks Bug, "Where do you live?"

Bug, still not knowing who Hunter is, replies, "Why do you need to know where I live? I thought you said you were my best friend. Shouldn't you know where I live?"

Hunter stops and looks Bug in the eyes. "Okay, I'm going to give you the short version. In the Horizon, where we became friends, we both had passed or nearly passed on to get there. You jumped to your demise, and I perished in a car accident. We became friends and battled the Jokers, Shadows, and monsters called the Hereafter Horde. You were a watcher for the warrior named Kannon. A watcher was like a bodyguard. I was a warrior; my sister was a watcher. There were three other warriors and watchers. Our job was to protect the four kings and lead them back to their thrones. You carried a bat named Babe. You became quite a fighter and fell in love with a girl named Spin Doll. Spin Doll was kidnapped and brought through her door in search of a baby named Bee. I've returned through your door to save you and take you with me to save them."

Puzzled, Bug asks, "So why my house? Why don't we just go to the door?"

"In the Horizon, we were told that the school planned a graduation party at your house to surprise you. I want to see if it's true."

Bug smiles. "They're having a party for me. That doesn't sound right. You sure you got the right guy?"

Hunter sighs. "Just show me your house."

Bug says hesitantly, "Okay, but you've got the wrong guy."

Cars line both sides of Bug's street as he runs home, smiling. Cougar's truck is parked nearby, and Hunter and Bug join a crowd of classmates in his yard—including his crush, Becky Jones. The group greets Bug with claps and cheers.

Cougar puts his arm around Bug's shoulders. "This is all for you, Bug Boy."

Sitting at a long table is Bug's untouched diploma and a large cake that reads "Congrats, Bug Boy."

Bug can't believe they're all there for him. All through school they were mean and rude to him. He was bullied by them since seventh grade. But now… this.

Cougar motions for the crowd to quiet down. "Bug, this cake is for you. This is for all the hard work you completed. Enjoy, Bug Boy. Here, let me cut you the first piece."

Hunter is happy to be able to watch his friend get honored by his peers.

Becky begins to chant, "Bug, Bug, Bug, eat that cake!"

Hunter wonders why they're all focused so much on cake. Then Cougar cuts a large piece and hands it to Bug, the crowd still chanting, "Eat the cake, eat the cake, eat the cake."

Bug accepts his piece and holds it up along with a fork. The crowd cheers louder. Hunter feels something is up, but what, he doesn't quite know. Bug takes a big forkful and shoves it in his mouth but quickly spits it out while trying to wipe off his tongue. The crowd erupts in laughter.

Cougar yells, "Hope you loved the cake. Our dogs made it!"

Bug gags and screams, "You fed me dog shit? Why would you do that?"

Hunter approaches Cougar, and the crowd goes silent to listen. "Now you take a bite."

Cougar looks at Hunter and chuckles. "Who are you, mister? This doesn't concern you. Unless you'd also like some cake."

Hunter says angrily, "Take a bite! Last time I say it."

Bug continues spitting as he works his way between the two and holds his hands up. "You know you don't have to get involved. This happens all the time; it's nothing new."

Hunter looks at Bug, not believing what he's hearing. "Really, you're going to let this slide. The Bug I remember would've tea-bagged this clown."

Bug shrugs and offers a weak smile. "Trust me, if we don't stop here, it will only get worse."

Hunter narrows his eyes. "Oh, it's about to get worse."

Cougar laughs at that remark as he pulls his shirt off and hollers, "Bug Boy, I don't think your friend here knows the pecking order! Buddy, someone's going to eat cake. But it definitely isn't going to be me."

Bug turns toward Cougar and tries to calm the situation down. "Cougar, I don't think we need anyone to eat this cake. Let's just party and enjoy ourselves."

Cougar pushes Bug back a few steps. "How about you try another piece, Bug boy?"

"Cougar, really, this is not a good time for this. Emotions are high, and hey, we're all adults here," Bug nervously explains.

Cougar chuckles as he pushes Bug again. "I said, eat another piece of cake. Or do you need me to feed it to you?"

Becky yells from the back, "Make him eat another piece of dog shit cake!" Bug is shocked and disappointed to hear that come from her mouth. All this time, he thought she liked him.

Hunter leans down and whispers, "You want me to handle this guy?"

Bug smiles. "Nah, I got this. What? Do you think I can't handle my own fights?" He sticks his hand out as Hunter pulls Babe out of his pack.

Cougar laughs. "Oh no, Bug Boy has a bat. Drop it before I shove it up your ass and make you look like a corndog."

Bug narrows his eyes. "I think your mouth just wrote me a check your ass can't cover."

Hunter smiles as he steps back, knowing what version of Bug that Cougar is about to meet.

Cougar yells, "C'mon, Bug Boy! You want some; come get some."

Bug takes a step toward Cougar. "For six years you bullied me, called me names, knocked me down, and were pretty much a dickhead. But now we're no longer in school. We're adults. I know Becky will probably sleep with all the new twelfth graders, since she already has most of ours. But today, today is a little different. Today you'll learn how to talk to a man correctly."

Cougar swings at Bug, who ducks and cracks Cougar in the mouth, releasing two teeth. Bug growls, "Now, this isn't over till you try a piece of my cake. I'm sure with more room in your mouth now, you can fit more in."

Cougar falls to the ground, holding his mouth with one hand and trying to pick up his teeth with the other. Bug steps on his hand as he punches Cougar in the face, releasing another tooth.

A voice from the crowd yells, "That's enough! Let him up."

Hunter looks at the crowd. "It's enough when Bug says it's enough. One more person opens their fucking mouth, and you all will eat a piece of cake."

The crowd doesn't respond as they back up.

Bug asks Cougar, "Now, where's all that backup you always have with you? Funny how none of those bitches will help you pick up your teeth."

Cougar, bleeding from the mouth and crying, begs, "Please, Bug, I'll never bother you again. I'm sorry."

"Well, I'll tell you what—you eat a big piece of cake, and I'll forget anything ever happened. Let's just say for every minute I wait, I'll extract another tooth."

Cougar quickly crawls to the table and begins eating a piece of cake, gagging the whole time.

Bug walks over to Becky and gives her a deep kiss. Then he walks away, laughing. "You only wish, *bitch.*"

Hunter smiles and addresses the crowd. "Thanks for the invite; had a blast. Feel free to stay as long as you like. Oh yeah and try some cake. Cougar recommends it." Then he catches up to an already-leaving Bug, who holds up both middle fingers as he leaves the group.

Bug jokes, "I'm a better hitter than I thought. I went for a single and ended up with a double."

They both laugh as Hunter adds, "Glad you're back, buddy."

Bug smiles. "I never left. But really, thanks for coming to get me. Now let's go find Spin Doll."

Walking a little taller, they head back for the door.

Chapter 9

"Ain't no hole big enough to hold that much greatness."
–The Jokers

Sin and Omin grumble and bicker from the moment they're thrown in the hole. Sitting in the dark for the last twenty-four hours makes the Jokers even madder than losing the war.

"Brother, nice call on teaming up with Father Time and that backstabbing hungry hippo," Sin complains.

"Let's give the other side the last piece of heart. What could it hurt?" Omin shoots back.

"Oh, really? And whose big idea was it to recruit the Hereafter Horde? Because that mercenary army really stuck around when things got tough, didn't they?" Sin grumbles.

"Let's get some company for our pet dragon. What's the worst that can happen? It gets loose and grows ten times its size. Oh yeah, and spits fire." Omin snorts back.

Sin calls truce. "Okay, enough. Let's just both agree you messed up and move on from it." He holds his hand out. "Brothers?"

Omin shakes his hand. "Brothers! At least now we can move on knowing you dropped the ball."

The two sit in silence, staring up the hole at the two angel guards.

"Hey, gentlemen, I need to go to the bathroom!" Sin yells up to them.

One of the angels says, "Use the corner on the right."

Sin, not thinking the response was funny, continues. "But I have to take a number two."

The other angel replies, "Oh, then use the left corner."

The Jokers hear the angels laughing at them.

Sin begins undoing his pants, and Omin says, "Whoa, whoa, whoa, what do you think you're doing?"

"I just said I have to take a number two!" Sin yells.

Omin, with a disgusted look on his face, says, "Well, not in this hole! I'm not smelling that the whole time we're down here."

"Unless you have a better option, you're going to have to live with it"

Before they can finish the new argument, a new voice is heard above. The strange but familiar voice speaks to the angels. "I'm here to relieve one of you. Whichever one it is, the kings would like to see you immediately."

The two angels play odds or evens for the right to leave. The winner turns over his spot to the new voice.

"Oh, great, a shift change. Just when we're starting to connect," Sin sarcastically jokes.

Omin tries to speak but is interrupted by a falling angel's body hitting the hole's floor, then the light orb pops out. The two Jokers stare at each other, trying to figure out what just happened. They look to the top of the hole and see a familiar face.

"Cozzex!" Sin and Omin yell at the same time.

Cozzex yells down to them, "Are you two just gonna hang out down there, or are we getting those thrones back?"

"Get us out of here!" the brothers scream.

Cozzex throws down a rope. "Your plan worked perfectly. That old idiot really thought you two released your own sister."

"That definitely was one of your best performances. Kudos, sis," Omin replies.

"You left us sitting down in that hole for almost twenty-four hours. I almost shit down there," Sin complains.

"Yeah, yeah, if you'd stop your bitching for one minute, I'll explain why." Once they're both out of the hole, Sin and Omin gesture that the floor is all hers. "I just couldn't run in here all willy-nilly. Three angels were released for this plan to take place."

"Three? Why three? The one you shape-shifted into and one you shoved down the hole," Sin interrupts.

Cozzex glares, causing Sin to close his mouth. "For some reason, King Dayne walked out. This drew attention away from your prison. Why are there so many holes in the Horizon? No matter what, I had a short window, and I took it. So maybe we shouldn't hang out in the open bullshitting."

The Jokers agree as they creep out of sight.

* * *

Dak enters the kingdom, saddened by his friend's decision to depart the Horizon. Instantly upon his arrival, he's informed that his mother is nowhere to be found. One of the angels' reports, "Sir, your mother has gone missing. She was sitting on her throne, handing out judgments, then she was gone. We've checked the kingdom and have not seen hide nor hair of her."

"Well, then search again. She must be found," Dak orders.

The angels once again begin looking through the kingdom, turning the place upside down. The search party is interrupted by two screaming angels. Dak immediately approaches them, hoping they'd found his mother.

The out-of-breath angels try to speak, then one blurts out, "Sir, the prisoners have escaped!"

"The prisoners have escaped. How could this happen? They couldn't have just jumped out. It's been less than a day."

Dak instantly thinks the Jokers have taken his mother. He assembles their small armies of angels, sending them west, south, and north. Dak, by himself, heads east. His only orders are to dispose of all Shadows and return his mother. Before he leaves, he approaches the three kings.

"My kings, we are off to find my mother, the fourth king. Would any of you like to accompany me?"

Truncheon speaks. "I should say not. I have my own business to tend to here."

"A search party is no job for a king," Furrow agrees.

"Searching is beneath a king. Our time will be kept inside the kingdom walls from now on," Paragon also replies.

Dak, somewhat surprised, asks, "Aren't you at all worried something may happen to her, and you will again lose your power?"

"My boy, the Shadows are but a few now. Our worries are no more. With or without your mother, we'll never be without our thrones again," Paragon answers.

"Leave many an angel to protect us, and do not be gone long. We can't have the marked angel gallivanting around the countryside, especially with the Jokers on the loose again," Truncheon orders.

"A few hours, my boy, then you must return. She's a big girl; she can handle herself. Dilly-dally too long, and your services may be revoked," Furrow adds.

Dak is amazed at how uncaring the kings are. They're acting like spoiled, pompous asses.

Dak bows, then is off to find his mother and possibly the Jokers. He still can't believe the actions of the kings. As he forges off into the forest, he has a strange feeling that he isn't alone. Looking back every so often to see if he's being followed, seeing nothing, he shakes the paranoia from himself and focuses on finding his mother.

Chapter 10

"Ahhhh! The fine fickle finger of fate once again revisits us."
–Cam

Hunter and Bug return to the door to the Horizon. Hunter opens the door with the key and steps through, but Bug stands hesitantly, staring.

Hunter steps back through. "What are you doing? Let's go—we don't have much time."

Bug still doesn't move. "Is it going to hurt? What if I step through and die? I mean, I'm dead—released—over there."

"Didn't you already try to end yourself here?" Hunter asks.

"You know, you're right. Fuck it. Here goes nothing," Bug says, trying to talk himself into entering the door.

Hunter gestures toward the door as Bug runs and jumps through. Hunter follows, closing the door behind him.

Bug rolls across the floor and ends up on his back with his eyes closed. "Did we make it?"

Hunter laughs. "Get up, stupid. We made it. I told you we're just stepping through a door."

Bug opens his eyes. "Wow, the Horizon looks like shit. Not what I was picturing at all."

Hunter chuckles. "This is a cave. The Horizon is out there."

Bug opens the cave door. "Now this is more like it."

Before he can finish, Hunter yells, "Hey, that's later! Right now, we've got a job to do."

Bug closes the door and returns to Hunter, standing in front of the line of doors.

"How do you know which door is which? They all kind of look the same."

Hunter points at Spin Doll's door. "That's where we have to go.

But I'm thinking maybe we should get one more friend to even out the odds."

"I'm in. How do we pick the door?"

Hunter shrugs. "No idea. I guess we just cross our fingers and enter one."

"How about this one? It's green, and green is my third favorite color."

Hunter looks at the door Bug is pointing at and laughs. "Okay, let's take the green one."

When they enter, they find themselves standing in a hospital wing.

"Whoa, it's a hospital," Bug states.

Hunter knows right away whose door this is. He walks up to the first hospital desk they can find.

The nurse behind the counter asks, "Are you boys lost? Can I help you?"

"Yes, we're looking for our friend, Cam," Hunter explains.

The nurse smiles. "Does your friend Cam have a last name?"

Bug jumps in. "I'm sure he does, but we just don't know it."

"I believe he's in the cancer unit," Hunter continues.

The nurse checks her computer. After a few minutes, she responds, "Well, I only have one Cam. Does Cam Carleson sound like him?"

Bug, not knowing if it's him or not, responds before Hunter can. "Yeah, C.C., that's him. We're so used to calling him C.C."

The nurse points down the hall. "Down the hall, take a right, and go through the double doors. He's in Room 408."

Hunter thanks her, then the two head down the hall. Before they reach Cam's room, Hunter tells Bug, "Now, like you, Cam might not know us. So, let's approach him with kid gloves."

Bug agrees. The two take a deep breath and enter. Cam lies in the bed with an IV in his arm and his eyes closed.

Bug whispers, "Looks like he's dead, is this the Cam we're looking for?"

Hunter nods as he stands beside Cam's bed. Quietly, they stand, not wanting to touch him.

The door swings open as a woman in her early forties walks in. Startled, she asks, "Who are you?"

"Hi, I'm Hunter, and this is Bug. We're friends of Cam's," Hunter answers softly.

"Really? Cam never mentioned having friends."

"It's true, we're his friends," Bug replies backing up Hunter.

The lady breaks down into tears. Hunter, not knowing what else to do, hugs her, "Ma'am, are you all right?"

She wipes her tears. "He'll be so glad you're here. Nobody has ever come to see him before. I'm just shocked that he has friends. How are you friends? Oh, never mind, I'm just so happy he's got friends. Thank you, boys. This is exactly what he needs." She hugs them both, then leaves the room to give them some time with Cam.

The two stand, watching Cam sleep. To their surprise, Cam speaks without opening his eyes. "So, my friends—is that what you're going with? Mom might be gullible, but I'm not. What do you want?"

Bug smiles and shouts, "Cam, you're alive! It's us—Bug and Hunter."

Cam opens his eyes. "Bug, Hunter, it's really you!"

"Now you're just playing with us. You have no clue who we are, do you?" Hunter asks.

Cam replies sarcastically, "Well, since I've never seen you before, I'm going to say no. I don't know you."

Bug explains excitedly, "I'm Bug. You and I distracted the witch so the others could take out the Beast. We're heroes!"

Cam looks at Hunter. "Either I'm on some really good meds, or he is."

Hunter gets a chair and sits beside Cam's bed. "We really don't have much time."

Cam interrupts. "You're telling me. The doctor just told me I may have up to a week left."

Hunter and Bug can't tell if Cam is serious or joking. "We need your help to save Spin Doll."

Cam interrupts again. "That's funny. You need my help. Look at me—does it look like I'm helping anyone?"

"Listen, I'm serious! You need to help us save Spin Doll from Jim and Hangman. We can't do it on our own," Hunter says, frustrated.

"Look, buddy, I don't know if you got the wrong room or something, but trust me, I ain't your guy."

"Can I hit him? Because someone in this room needs an ass beating," Bug retorts.

Cam laughs. "I may be sick and weak, but you're gonna need someone bigger than you, Bug, to kick my ass."

Bug goes from zero to angry in Bug fashion as he pulls up his sleeves and heads toward Cam. "That's it, bed bitch. Prepare for an ass-whipping of great proportions."

Hunter grabs Bug, while Cam begins to unhook himself from all his wires. "Bug, you go get a wheelchair. Cam, you get all unhooked. Guys, we're going Hangman hunting," Hunter orders both in a low tone.

Bug leaves the room by shoving the door open, while Cam lies back in his bed. With a huge smile, Cam says, "Man, that was so much fun. It's way too easy to get Bug fired up."

Hunter looks at Cam curiously. "Have you known who we were this whole time?"

"Of course. Who would ever forget the great Hunter?"

Hunter smiles now, knowing how much fun they're going to have with Bug.

Bug approaches the nurse who gave them the directions to Cam's room and asks, trying to be manly, "Beautiful, by any chance, do you happen to know where I might locate a wheelchair?"

She points across the waiting room and, without looking up, replies, "You mean all those chairs with wheels on them?"

Bug is not amused. "You mind if I borrow one?"

The nurse, still looking down at her screen, replies, "Feel free, handsome. Just let me know if you need help pushing it."

Bug, still not amused, walks over and grabs a wheelchair. Walking by the nurse, he asks, "Don't you want to know why I need it?"

The nurse finally looks up, realizing he's not going to leave her alone. "Why do you need the wheelchair?"

Bug smiles. "I'll tell you if you give me your phone number."

The nurse looks back at the screen. "Well then, I guess neither of us is getting what we want today."

Bug turns and walks away, pushing the wheelchair. "Oh, don't worry—you'll miss me."

She simply replies, "With every shot I take." Then she makes a finger gun gesture towards him.

When Bug reaches the room, Cam sits waiting with all his wires unhooked. He quickly explains, "We better hurry. They'll be coming in to check why my wires are off."

Bug pulls the wheelchair up to the bed. "Your chariot awaits, Sir Cam."

"How about letting the big guy push me. I'd like to get there in one piece," Cam replies jokingly.

Bug, straining a little, looks at Hunter and whispers, "He's all yours. Feel free to push him off a cliff, for all I care. I don't think I care too much for this version of Cam."

Hunter plays referee as he tries to calm Bug down.

"Hey, little guy, you should probably walk behind us. Wouldn't want you getting run over," Cam continues.

"Have you ever gotten your ass beat while in a wheelchair?" Bug grumbles.

"Nope, and I'm not worried about it today either," Cam barks back.

Without being seen, Hunter finally gets the bickering two to the door.

"Well, this is the end of your ride. You're gonna have to walk the rest of the way," Hunter explains to Cam. Hunter and Bug help Cam to his feet.

Once standing, Cam says, "Shit, I really am taller than you. Bet you were a four-year T-ball player, weren't you?"

Hunter gives Bug the "just ignore him" look as the men walk through the door.

Chapter 11

"When the hangman comes calling, pretend no one is home."
–Spin Doll

Spin Doll lies next to Bee, half asleep, trying to keep her eyes open. Jax sits in a big comfy chair, drawing, and Diesel is lying in a pile of old blankets on the floor. Suddenly, Diesel looks up toward the door, hearing something the others can't. Diesel's ears are on end, and now they can hear footsteps. Whoever it is, it sounds like they are looking for something. The footsteps stop in front of their door. No one in the room makes a sound. They remain silent even when they hear a knock.

Jax pushes Diesel's blanket pile to the side, revealing a trap door. Quickly, Spin Doll grabs Bee and enters the hole, then Jax covers the door with the blanket pile.

A louder knock this time. Diesel begins to growl as the knock turns into pounding.

"Spin Doll, I know you're in there. Open the door!"

It's Jim's voice.

Jax replies, "There's no Spin Doll in here, just me and my large, mean dog." A hand punches through the locked door, followed by an eyeball peering through.

Once again Jim speaks, "Don't lie to me, little girl; I know she's in there."

An arm comes through the hole, trying to unlock the door. Diesel leaps and grabs it, ripping it away from the locks. Jim yells in pain as he tries to pull his arm back out of the hole. Jax and Diesel can hear Jim complaining in the hallway as he orders Hangman to break the door down. The door doesn't stand a chance against Hangman, and soon they enter the room.

The four stand mere feet from each other, sizing each other up.

Jim says, "Now, little girl, don't get yourself hurt for Spin Doll. I'm sure she wouldn't do the same for you."

Jax doesn't respond. Spin Doll can hear every word Jim is saying while she lies with Bee in the hidden hole.

Jim points at Diesel and says, "Now that was a very bad dog. Do you know what we do to bad dogs?" He gestures to Hangman to punish Diesel. Diesel puts up much more of a fight than either expected. The Hangman and Diesel roll around on the ground, fighting with everything they have. It is so evenly matched, no one can tell which one is winning.

Finally, Hangman receives a break as Diesel falls into a coffee table, stunning himself for a second. The Hangman wrestles him from behind in a chokehold. Diesel fights to get loose, but to no avail. Soon Diesel passes out from lack of oxygen. The Hangman drags the limp body over to the window and tosses Diesel out. They all can hear a thud as Diesel's body hits the ground from the three-story fall.

Jax wants to run to the window to help her friend, but, outnumbered two to one, she searches for an escape route instead. The building is quite old and has an old laundry chute that leads to the basement. Luckily enough for her, she can fit. She dives into it, falling to the basement, landing in a pile of old, musty, mildew-covered sheets. Jax looks up at the shoot to see Jim looking down at her. She flips him off and quickly makes her escape.

Bee begins to fuss a little, almost giving away their hiding spot, but Spin Doll quickly gets him to calm down.

Jim stomps back and forth across the floor, furious that Spin Doll slipped from his fingers once again. He yells at Hangman, "How do we lose them again? When we eventually catch them and just end Spin Doll's life? She is of no importance to us. Now the little baby, Bee, I know three who would like to meet him. That is, before we dispose of him as well."

Jim laughs at his own words as the two men head out the door to the basement. When Spin Doll is sure the coast is clear, she and Bee climb out of the hidden trap door. Carrying Bee, Spin Doll rushes to the broken window and down at the street, looking at a lifeless Diesel. Glass and blood surround him. Spin Doll watches for any movement but there isn't any.

"Another soul was lost, trying to protect me. Maybe I should just give up and save my remaining friends," she whispers to Bee. Covering the little baby, Spin Doll and Bee leave the room in search of a new safe place.

Jax makes her way out of the basement before Jim and Hangman can get to her, but reaching the street, she stops dead in her tracks. The sight of her best friend lying there is more than she can handle. She sits on the curb with Diesel lying in front of her, and she can no longer hold the tears back. Her best friend is right here, and she can't do anything to save him. No longer caring if she is caught by Jim, she covers her face with her arms.

Suddenly, a kind voice speaks from the air. "You know, they say a dog is more than a pet. They can be your best friend, family, protector, and, to some, emotional support. I'm sure he was all of the above."

Jax doesn't look up as she says, "He is my only family. This world never stops being hard. I have had so much sorrow; I can't even make a smile anymore."

Cam appears, sitting beside her, and places his arm around her shoulder. "Smiles are overrated and seem to only be used by evil. Now, those tears that are falling from your eyes… those are real. Real is the only thing that can heal a broken heart."

Jax looks up at him. "Sadness seems to be the only emotion I have left. I don't think this world wants me anymore. And, even if it does, I don't think *I* want it anymore."

Cam hugs her tighter. "This world might not want you, but we sure do. My name is Cam, and I could use another friend. Plus, there's always room in our family for one more. Someday, when you're feeling more like talking, you can tell us about your best friend right here. Now, if you'd like, my friends and I will help get your friend out of the street. We most definitely do not want anyone remembering him this way."

Cam helps Jax to her feet, leading her to the sidewalk. Then he rips off a small piece of his shirt and hands it to Jax to wipe her eyes with.

"My lady, I am proud to introduce you to—"

"Well, well, well, if it isn't Mr. Ill, I need a pill. What brings you to our cozy little city?" Jim chuckles. "No matter, we have business with this pretty little lady. So why don't you vanish? I hear you are good at that. Or maybe you want to go take a nap. I hear you are good at that as well."

"Jim, I'm surprised to see you. Well, maybe I'm not, since there are so many park benches around here. Isn't it almost dinner time with your brother? I apologize; that was very fat—I mean bad of me."

Jim's face turns as red as the broken stop sign at the end of the street. With anger in his eyes, he states, "Cam, I'd like you to meet my friend. We call him Hangman."

"Pleased to meet you. Sorry, I'm not a handshaker. But, while we're introducing friends, allow me to introduce Hunter and Bug."

Hunter and Bug step from around the corner. Jim's eyes widen, and he takes a step back toward Hangman.

Hunter and Bug walk up beside Cam and Jax, and Hunter asks, "Jim, do we seem to have a problem here?"

Jim smiles. "Well, it seems as though some of us are about to have a problem. Fellas, let me introduce you to Mr. Hangman."

Bug nods. "Hangman, ha. Well, Mr. Hangman, let me introduce my foot and your ass. The way I look at it, you only get three strikes. The first strike was hanging out with this little piece of shit. The second strike was throwing a dog out a window. I mean, who does that? The third strike was involving me."

Bug pulls his bat back as Cam disappears, and Hunter pulls out his pool stick.

Jim raises his hands and yells, "Now, now, can't we get along for a minute? Hear me out. We came here to get little Bee. Once we have the Bee, we'll leave. No sense in all this fighting all the time."

Jax yells back, "You'll never get Bee, you sick bastard!"

Hunter shakes his head. "Sounds like you're not getting this Bee you're looking for. But please, allow me to show you the door."

Hunter begins sending shot after shot into Hangman's body, which sends Hangman reeling backwards. Bug slides on his knees and swings his bat, taking out Hangman's knees and sending him face first to the ground. Bug and Hunter high-five, feeling good about themselves.

Bug happily touts, "Is that the best you have? Jim, you better hope your bullpen is better than that."

Jim smiles and tells the two cocky men, "Oh, that was just the first inning. You see, my starter gets stronger as more pain is inflicted on him. The more you hurt him, the stronger he gets."

Hunter and Bug's smiles now vanish as Hangman sits up.

Cam takes Jax's hand and yells, "Let's go; this battle will have to be another day!"

The two run down the street and around the corner. Hunter and Bug attack once again, leaving Hangman face down. Like last time, Hangman sits up.

Jim laughs and cheers. "That's it, guys. Make him stronger. It's like we're a team."

Hunter, confused, orders Bug to get back. We'll have to fall back and continue this another day."

Bug nods and turns, then runs down the street in the same direction as Cam and Jax. Hunter turns toward Jim before running and shoots him in the left foot. Then, as he runs away, Hunter yells, "Now, old man, you have something in common with your fat brother!"

Jim rolls around on the ground, holding his blood-soaked shoe. The Hangman stands and picks Jim up, carrying him like a baby down the street in the same direction as the fleeing four.

Chapter 12

"Have you ever met someone who knew you, but you had no idea who they were?" –Dayne

After making her way from the Kingdom, Dayne walks another two hours through the woods. She has never traveled this far alone before and is unfamiliar with the surroundings. Upon finding a clearing, she stops for a short break. She still can't stop thinking of Kannon's face in that bubble.

"How can the kings expect me to pass judgment on my husband and friends?" Dayne yells to the woods.

Exhausted, she lays back against an old tree stump, listening to the sounds of the forest.

Soon it'll be dark. Maybe I should build a fire and rest here for the night.

Dayne gathers some wood and soon has a fine fire. The warmth of the flames begin to make her eyes droopy, and in no time, she is fast asleep. Dreams fill her head.

She and Kannon, dancing in their special place at the top of the town.

Kannon's car radio repeatedly playing their wedding song, as fireflies dance along with the beat. Kannon twirls her around and around, taking her breath away as he refuses to stop.

Suddenly she is awakened by a snap of a twig coming the opposite side of the fire. Without moving, she peers through the flames into the woods.

A blurry figure appears, and the closer it comes, the clearer it becomes to Dayne.

"Excuse me, ma'am, would you be so kind to share your fire with an old, weary knight?" the man politely asks.

Standing in the light of the fire is a real knight with armor and a helmet, which he holds at his side.

"Sir, I don't usually share my fire with a stranger."

The knight bows his head. "Ma'am, my name is Willow. I am a knight of the Horizon. Now that you know me, I am no longer a stranger. I beg of you, just a quick nap in the warmth of your fire, then I will leave."

Hesitant about it, Dayne answers, "Willow, as long as you stay on that side of the fire, you may rest for a short time."

Willow thanks Dayne and quickly sits on his side of the fire.

The two sit in silence, staring at the flames.

Dayne finally speaks. "Willow, Knight of the Horizon, what brings you out in the woods all alone tonight?"

Willow pokes at the bottom of the fire with a stick, watching the ashes dance. "Well, ma'am, I'm on a mission. I have a package that must be delivered to a young lady."

"Does this young lady have a name?"

"Ma'am, I'm sorry, but that's information I can't give out."

Dayne is annoyed and barks out, "Willow, do you know who you're speaking to? When I ask a question, I expect an answer!"

"Ma'am, I'm sorry, but if you're not the queen of the Horizon, I cannot tell you my mission. Maybe I should be going." Willow stands and begins to gather his belongings.

Dayne also stands, displeased at Willow's answer. "Queen!" she shouts. "What do you mean, *queen*? There are no queens in the Horizon. There are only kings, and I happen to be one. My name is Dayne, first lady king of the Horizon."

The knight immediately drops to one knee. "My queen, forgive me. Until you stood in the flame's light, I did not know it was you. Please forgive me."

"As I said before, the Horizon has only kings. You must be mistaken or have been told untruths."

"I am sorry, my Queen, but it is you who has been told untruths. You *are* my queen. I have been sent to find you and return you to your kingdom. To prove my words, I have a gift for you. This gift can only be held by the queen." Willow reaches into the sack and pulls out a beautiful, gold chest, which is about the size of a shoe box.

Dayne stares at the object, amazed at how the flames make it sparkle. "If I'm not the queen you think I am, what would happen if I touch the chest?"

"If you are not my queen, the chest will turn black when you touch it, and then it can only be opened by pure evil. Meaning my travels and sacrifices have been for naught." Willow sets the gleaming chest at Dayne's feet, then backs away.

Dayne, mesmerized by the beauty of the chest, does not want to be the reason for the chest to turn evil.

"I'm sorry, but you have the wrong person. I am a *king* of the Horizon. The King of Hearts. I will not be the reason this chest becomes evil. You are mistaken."

"I beg you, my Queen, open the chest and prove me right. The Horizon needs their queen before all is lost."

Dayne sighs. "Ok, I will open the chest. But if you are wrong—"

"If I am wrong, the Horizon will perish."

Dayne nods and slowly reaches down. The closer she gets, the brighter the object becomes. Both her and Willow's eyes widen. Dayne's hands are trembling, and they both hold their breath. As soon as Dayne's fingers touch the chest, lights shoot from it like fireworks, followed by a blinding light that fills the surrounding sky.

When the light dies down, and the two get their vision back, Dayne is standing in a beautiful, gold-studded gown that shimmers with every little movement. The chest lays open at her feet.

Willow immediately drops to both knees and shouts, "my queen, you have returned!"

Dayne can feel enlightenment and freedom flow through her body, as if all her troubles have been lifted and everything is right. She looks down at the chest, but, surprisingly, there is nothing in it.

"The chest is empty."

Willow shakes his head. "Reach inside, my Queen. For only you can pull the item from the chest."

Dayne reaches into the empty chest to prove Willow wrong. But, when she does, an item appears as she pulls her hands from it. It is a round stone-like ball with diamonds encrusted around it.

Willow exclaims, "The legend is true! When the queen once again rises, so does her dragon."

"Are you saying this is a dragon's egg?"

"Indeed, it is my Queen. Indeed, it is."

Dayne reaches back into the chest and lifts the dragon egg from it. Holding it in the air, she spins it and lights dance from the fire's light.

"My apologies, my Queen, that I did not recognize you immediately."

"Willow, I forgive you. But even though I can hold the dragon's egg, I still find it hard to believe I'm a queen. If I'm a queen, where is my kingdom?"

"Why, the Northern Horizon is your kingdom, my lady."

Dayne's eyebrows furrow in confusion. "Where do I live?"

Willow chuckles, thinking the queen is messing with him. "You live in the Divine Castle, of course."

"The Divine Castle?"

Willow now realizes Dayne has no idea what he is talking about. He asks Dayne to sit so he can explain. Now, holding a dragon's egg and more intrigued than ever, Dayne quickly sits, and Willow tosses another log on the fire.

Chapter 13

"Some stories never get old." –Spin Doll

Spin Doll carries Bee for about ten blocks before entering what seems to be an abandoned grocery store. With no lights on, she waits till her eyes adjust to the darkness, then sets Bee down and lets him walk on his own. Aisle after aisle, they walk, searching for food left on the shelves. They recover three cans of pork and beans, an unopened box of Jello, and a half full jug of fruit juice. Quietly, they sit and eat the beans. Spin Doll is grateful that the cans are pop tops and don't need a can opener. After eating their fill of beans, Spin Doll has to find something to clean Bee up with, since it looks as if he took a bath in the beans instead of eating them. Once Bee is cleaned, Spin Doll takes the boy and hides in the cooler so she can see everything through the glass doors.

While sitting there trying to be quiet, Spin Doll, whispering, tells Bee a story. "Once upon a time, there was a dragon that had no friends. The dragon searched high and low for anyone who could use a friend. He found some campers trying to start their campfire. He knew starting fires was one thing he was good at. So, he blew fire from his mouth at the pile of sticks in the fire ring. Instantly, the sticks caught, making the campfire pop and crackle. Happy he could help, the dragon thought that would get him a friend. But it doesn't, as all the campers ran away. The dragon was even sadder now than he was before. He took to the air and soared sadly over the treetops. Thinking he would find a friend, he decided to keep flying until he disappeared for good.

"Soaring high over the land, he suddenly heard a cry for help. Reaching the voice, he noticed a young boy hanging from a cliff. The boy wasn't going to hold on much longer; he was certain to fall to his doom. The dragon flew down the cliffside, just catching the young boy as he lost his grip. The dragon flew them both to the bottom of the mountain and set him down. With a thud, the boy dropped to the ground. The dragon noticed the boy acted differently from the people he had met before. The boy did not run from him, nor did he scream. Instead, he said, 'Thank you so much. You saved my life. My name is Jake. I am pleased to meet you.' The dragon looked around to see if the boy might be speaking to someone else. Not seeing anyone else, the dragon knew the boy must be talking to him.

"The dragon fist bumped the boy and said, 'You're welcome, Jake.' Jake smiled and replied, 'What's your name? As you can see, I'm blind. Some mean kids led me to the ridge and told me it was a slide. I believed them, thinking maybe I had some new friends. But, like everyone else, they made fun of me because I was different. Do you have any friends, because if you don't, I'd like to be your friend?' That brought a smile to the dragon's face, and he replied, 'Well, I have a lot of friends already.' The boy's face lost its happy emotion. The dragon continued. 'But I don't see why I can't have another friend. Yeah, I will be your friend.' Jake jumped with happiness, excited to finally have a friend. Jake couldn't tell, but the dragon was just as happy. The two danced around in a circle. Once they stopped dancing, they walked to the creek and threw rocks in to see who could make the biggest splash.

"Jake listened to his rocks make a plop sound as they hit the water. He joked, 'Did you hear that splash? Bet you can't beat that. Hey, what's your name?' The dragon said, 'My name is Torch.' Jake laughed and said, 'Well, Torch, I bet you can't beat this splash.' Jake threw a decent-sized rock into the water. Torch picked out a rock bigger than Jake's and tossed it into the creek. The splash from the rock flew back toward the two, leaving them both drenched. Jake, still grinning, yelled, 'Wow, I guess you won! Good job, friend.' Torch smiled, hoping the day would never end. He was not going to tell Jake he was a dragon in fear that he'd lose another friend. Torch kept his distance and only fist-bumped Jake when something was cool.

"The two play till night came. Torch built a roaring fire and found some food for them to eat. They laughed and told jokes that were not that funny to one another. Neither of them, wanting the day to end, agreed to tell each other a secret they'd been hiding. Torch went first, thinking of something other than he was a dragon. 'Well, Jake, my secret is that I have never had a friend before.' Jake smiled and replied, 'Well, you can't say that anymore, friend. Now for my secret.' Jake paused, thinking for a minute. 'My secret is that I never had a dragon as a friend.' Torch's smile dropped as he blurted, 'You knew I was a dragon? How? You can't see.' Jake laughed. 'Well, I was falling, and you caught me, then slowly you floated to the ground. Next, you covered us with water from the huge rock you threw in. Finally, I felt the heat as you started the fire instantly. Who else could do all that but a dragon?' Torch sadly stood, preparing to leave. Jake asked if he was leaving, and Torch explained that every time he tried to make a friend, they got scared and ran away. Jake said he'd never run away and told Torch how cool it was to have a dragon for a friend! 'Sorry, but you're stuck with me, big guy,' Jake said. Torch was excited but afraid to believe it. Jake assured him that his best friend was a dragon. The new friends sat and talked throughout the night."

Spin Doll's story ends and she notices Baby Bee is fast asleep, so she lays him down. As she turns around, she is greeted by a familiar voice.

"So, what's the moral of the story?"

Spin Doll smiles at Bug and hugs him, almost smothering him. Hunter laughs as he adds, "Hey, save some of that hug for me." Spin Doll reaches over and pulls Hunter into her and Bug's hug.

Then Bug says, "No, really, what's the point of the story?"

Spin Doll smiles. "A true friend can see the real you."

Chapter 14

"My king is a queen." –Dak

Willow sits across from the queen. "My queen, you rule the northern part of the Horizon, known to all as Paradise. The only entrance is at your command. If you allow the gates of pearls to open, they may enter. Once inside, they cannot return."

Dayne, surprised, thinks the kingdom is all the Horizon with bits of here surrounding it. "How large is this Paradise?"

"Massive. It travels for miles."

"If no one can leave Paradise, why are you here?"

"Because I'm one of the seven."

"Seven what?"

"One of the seven Knights of Paradise. These knights may travel outside Paradise only when the queen is beyond its walls or she grants us permission. With you lost in the Horizon, we had to search."

"Besides you and me seven, who else can leave?"

Willow pauses. "Your friend and second in command, Owl. There is one other..."

Brush rustles from the left as Willow draws his sword and stands in front of his queen. Dak emerges from the bushes. "Mother, are you alright?"

"Back! I said back!"

Dak draws his sword as Willow's eyes widen. "It's you, the marked angel. My queen, I will protect you."

"Willow, this is my son, Dak. Put your sword down."

"Mom, who is this man? Are you okay?" Dak confusingly asks.

"Today will not be my release. Drop your sword, then to your knees, marked angel!" Willow shouts.

Dayne orders both men to lower their weapons, but neither do.

Willow whistles an eerie melody. Soon, Dak is surrounded by more knights, all pointing their swords at him.

"Marked Angel, I will tell you once more. Drop the sword and fall to your knees," Willow now angrily insists.

Dak realizes he's outnumbered by more than Shadows, drops his sword, and falls to his knees. The knights quickly tie his hands and feet. After tossing his sword in the bushes, they sit him in front of the fire. A knight stands behind him on each side.

"What is the meaning of this? This is my son. I demand you release him immediately!" Dayne orders.

"My queen, this is your son. But he's also the marked angel. You asked who can come and go from Paradise. Your seven knights, Owl, and the marked angel. This man was tossed from Paradise by your orders. Due to his heinous act inside Paradise, you marked him and forced him to leave."

"Why would I ever banish my son?" Dayne startlingly questions.

"Because he let the monster into Paradise. The monster who stole the stars and the baby storyteller. The monster poisoned the baby, which changed many stories. The marked angel has been banished until he returns the baby and fixes the wronged stories," Willow replies.

"Mom, it's got to be a lie. There are no children in the Horizon. Did you not see how rapidly I've grown? You're my mother. Do you really think I could hurt you?" Dak begs for her side.

Dayne is as confused as Dak. She sits back in her place, wondering if this is true.

"My queen, allow me to acquaint you with our other six knights. First, we have Chet, the strongest of the seven and deadliest with a sword. Next is Russell, a bit of a jokester, but in battle, he's all business. This is Maverick, our marksman. No one is more accurate with a crossbow. These two are the brothers of precision. Being twins, they know each other's moves. Imagine fighting two of the exact same fighters. They move in unison. The one on the left is Nene, and the one on the right is Meme. Finally, this is Megan. She's what we call the silent assassin. Her moves are as beautiful as she is. And I, my lady, am Willow, as I explained earlier."

"Why should we believe you're good guys? You might be working for the Jokers!" Dak yells.

Willow turns toward Dak. "What is this about Jokers?"

"Don't play stupid! You know who the Jokers are. The kings will send help soon, then we'll see where your loyalty lies," Dak meanly informs the knights.

"Kings? What do you mean, kings? There is only one king in the Horizon. The King of Refuged.

"There are four kings. I know this because we helped them regain the kingdom from the Jokers," Dak boasts.

"These Jokers, do they have a name?" Chet asked.

"Sin and Omin, for Sinister and Ominous," Dak replies, as if they already know.

Willow smiles along with the rest of the knights. "Sinister and Ominous! That sounds like two brothers and a sister who were triplets. These three were in Paradise but came up missing. Rumor has it they snuck out to help find the queen and rescue her to gain a higher spot in the ranks. They mean well, but they're harmless."

"Harmless? They released my husband, Kannon," Dayne explains.

The knights all take to arms. "If King Kannon is here, we must get you back to Paradise immediately. It's not safe here."

"King Kannon? Kannon is not a king. I am a king, along with Furrow, Paragon, and Truncheon. We are the kings, not Kannon," Dayne insists.

"My queen, we know not of these other kings," all the knights together answer.

"We only know of King Kannon, the King of Refuged," Chet insists.

"My father is no king. He perished in the battle for the kingdom. Does that sound like a king to you?" Dak barks back at them.

The knights are all confused as they help Dak to his feet and gesture Dayne to follow. Willow leads the way into the woods, while Russell and Chet follow behind the group.

Chapter 15

"Help will come from the ones you least expect." –Mimic

Feigning exhaustion, the three kings leave their thrones for the night, agreeing to meet in an hour in the dungeons. The crowds disperse, leaving hundreds and thousands of light orbs floating in the sky. Even with the kings now in power, the stars have yet to return.

After an hour passes, the three kings meet in Octoro's former prison room. Making sure they aren't followed, they huddle in the corner of the dungeon.

"Brothers, the plan worked perfectly. As a matter of fact, it might have worked better than we planned," Paragon says.

"Letting the heroes release the Hereafter Horde was brilliant. There was no way we could have defeated them ourselves," Furrow adds.

Paragon laughs. "And to think, they blamed it all on those idiot Jokers. With Jim in another world and King Kannon now trapped in a sphere, who's to stop us? Once the queen is released, we'll have control of the entire Horizon." All three kings laugh at their success.

Little do they know, Mim and IC are listening to the whole conversation. The kings never look up, and Mimic hovers above them, hidden behind a statue that hangs on the wall.

"Hopefully we never see that Jim again. If we're so lucky, we'll lock him down here for eternity," Paragon continues.

"What if the stars return to the sky? All those who were released will return. Those warriors, King Kannon, and that lunatic Fat Jack will all return. How will we get them all in the cells?" Furrow asks.

Truncheon smiles as he points to Octoro's cell. "They'll all end up here. But don't worry, brothers, they will not return unless we return them."

"What's in the cell? Octoro is gone. We watched as he sank into the ground."

Truncheon opens the cell door, and the other two follow him in. Mimic tries to get a look, but their hiding spot won't allow it. Truncheon points to the corner of the cell to a spider nest that spans from floor to ceiling.

"Is that what I think it is?" Furrow asks.

Truncheon nods. "It sure is. Thousands of Octoros waiting to hatch."

Furrow steps back. "They'll destroy everything."

Truncheon holds up three little vials hooked to claws.

"What are those?" Paragon questions.

"Each one of these little bottles is filled with Octoro's blood. The babies will think we're Octoro. They'll follow us anywhere. Trust me, no one will dare get near us." Truncheon smiles, showing his dingy teeth.

"So, if everyone's gone, who are we going to be kings of? "Furrow asks.

"The spiders won't be able to enter Paradise without permission. So, they can have this place and feed on all the new lights that begin in here, while we live happily in charge of Paradise."

The kings laugh as they leave the cell and exit the dungeon.

Once the dungeon is clear, Mim and IC fly down into the cell. Getting a firsthand look at the spider nest, Mim says disgustedly, "We must find a way to destroy this nest. We need to get to Dayne."

IC, drawn to the nest, asks, "When will they hatch?"

Mim doesn't have a good feeling. "Let's get out of here. I don't want to be here when they hatch."

But before they can leave, the cell door slams shut, trapping the two with the soon-to-hatch spiders. The window in the cell door opens, drawing Mimic's attention.

"What do we have here?" a smiling king inquires.

"Looks like a couple of flies," the kings continue to joke.

"I wouldn't want to be a fly in a room full of spiders," Furrow adds.

"My kings, please let us out of here. We must get up to the stars and start cleaning!" Mim yells.

"Please, you need us. Who's going to teach the new cleaners how to clean?" IC adds.

"Not one of us gives a shit about those damn stars. Looks like this is the end, little flies," Truncheon states.

"But we took care of you in the hole. You owe us," Mimic together begs.

Paragon yells back, "You little bug, how dare you speak to your kings like that? You really think that was us in that hole? Those were some bums we let borrow our clothes. We told them they'd get to be kings for a day. Poor saps. They were pretty much dead in the hole. When Lakin and Jack started to fight, we released the fakes and replaced them. Did you really think we miraculously healed?"

The kings begin laughing as they shut the window and walk away.

Mim and IC hug, knowing that this is the end. They hover in front of the door with their eyes closed, waiting for the worst, as the sack begins to move and bulges appear from the baby spiders wanting out.

Suddenly, the cell door opens, and hands reach in to grab Mim and IC and pull them out. The door slams shut just as the spider nest looks as if it was about to bursts open.

Mim and IC still have their eyes closed, not knowing they've been saved.

"You can open your eyes, fireflies. You're safe for now."

Mim and IC slowly open their eyes to reveal the Jokers and Cozzex standing in front of them.

IC tries to yell, but Cozzex covers her mouth. "Shhh, you want to let the kings know we saved you?"

IC shakes her head.

"You guys were thrown in the hole," Mim whispers.

"Yeah, but our sister helped us escape. Now we're saving you two," Omin whispers.

"You're the bad guys. Why would you help us?" a frightened IC asks.

"Maybe we're not really the bad guys," Sin answers.

"But I watched you two release Kannon," Mim insists.

"Kannon wasn't a king. Dayne was," Omin continues.

Cozzex intervenes. "Kannon is a king. Actually, he's the only king. He's the King of the Refuged. Dayne, on the other hand, is the Queen of Paradise. Let's get out of here. We can explain later. I don't want to be anywhere near this door when it breaks."

The five quickly escape out the back, unseen by everyone.

Chapter 16

"When one door closes, lock that bitch." –Bug

Spin Doll lets go of Bug and Hunter when she notices Jax and Cam standing behind them.

"Cam, you're back."

Cam nods. "Yup, let's hope the third time's the charm. I'm kind of like a cockroach."

Spin Doll asks, "Jax, are you okay?"

Jax nods. "Yes. Your friends saved me."

Spin Doll hugs her. "I'm sorry you lost Diesel." Jax doesn't respond; she only nods.

Bug points out, "So this is the famous Baby Bee."

Hunter adds, "He does kind of look like you."

Spin Doll punches Hunter in the shoulder. "He's not my baby, idiot."

Bug shouts, "He's not? Then why's he so important to you?"

Spin Doll looks at Bee. "I don't know why. It just seems like I need to save him and return him to the Horizon."

Hunter says, "There are no kids in the Horizon. Won't he grow as soon as he enters it?"

Spin Doll shrugs. "He was brought to this world by a strange orb that set him in my arms as it explained I am the only one can hold the babe without seeing its story. Baby Bee was very ill. I cared for him for months, waiting for him to improve. Finally, the fever broke, and he quickly returned to the happy baby I'm guessing he was."

Jax adds, "Why does this old guy, Jim, want him so badly?"

Spin Doll shakes her head. "No idea, but he seems to think Bee is some storyteller."

Hunter holds up the one key. "Well, let's get Bee back home."

Bug reaches down and picks Bee up, then a vision runs through his mind, showing him explosions and turning every Shadow solid. Bug hands the baby to Spin Doll and walks away, looking as if he's seen a ghost.

Cam and Jax peek out of the store entrance, giving a thumbs up that the coast is clear. One by one, they exit the store. Hunter and Bug each pick a side and walk with Spin Doll and Bee between them. Cam and Jax continue ahead of them, looking out for any issues. Surprisingly, they make it back to the door. Looking around each side of the street, they stop behind a lone dumpster to regroup. Cam peers around the dumpster to see the lone door standing in the middle of an intersection.

Hunter whispers, "Cam, go invisible and make your way to the door. Once there, give us a thumbs-up if the coast is clear. Then, in single file, we'll quietly walk to the door."

They all agree with Hunter's plan, as Cam heads out to the door, and they watch quietly until Cam reappears and gives a thumbs-up. Jax leads the line, followed by Bug, Spin Doll, Bee, and Hunter. Reaching the door, Hunter pulls out the one key and pats Cam on the back. "Good job. Now let's get this door open and get out of here."

Cam turns to watch Hunter open the door.

They all stare at Cam as Bug asks, "Dude, you all, right?"

"Why? What do you mean?"

Hunter explains, "Cam, your nose and mouth are bleeding. Are you feeling good?"

Cam wipes his face with his hand and notices the blood. "Yeah, the doctors told me I had a few days left. Thinking now, those days might be up."

Spin Doll lowers Bee toward Cam, and Bee reaches out, placing his hand on Cam's face. Cam's vision leaves him as his mind places him back in his hospital bed. His parents stand beside his bed, holding each other. The doctors rush in and immediately begin working on him. Cam watches his soul leave his body and float above him. He can hear his mother praying as his dad hugs his mom. Concerned that his parents have been through too much with his sickness to keep them together, he intently watches as his father hugs his mom.

"Dear, he put up a hard fight. Now he may rest."

His mom cries, "What will we do without our little boy?"

"We will love each other enough to make up for Cam. I promise we'll be together forever."

Mom hugs Dad back. "The only thing he worried about was us, not his sickness."

Dad hugs her tighter. "Our love for each other was the only thing he shouldn't have worried about."

The doctor turns toward his parents, shaking his head as he turns off the machines.

Baby Bee removes his hand from Cam, and Cam returns to join them.

Bug asks, "Cam, are you all, right?"

Cam smiles. "Yes. Yes, I am."

Jim's voice interrupts the moment. "Well, well, what do we have here? It looks like you were about to leave without saying goodbye."

Hunter fumbles with the key as he tries unlocking the door but drops it, trying to rush.

Bug yells, "Stay back! We're leaving with or without you taking an ass-whooping."

Jim and Hangman begin walking toward them. Hunter retrieves the key and opens the door. Jax, Spin Doll, and Bee quickly go through as Hangman and Jim race toward them. Cam, Bug, and Hunter take their fighting stance. Closer and closer, the two bad men approach. Hunter grabs Bug and pushes him through the door. Hunter begins shooting to slow the charging men down and yells, "Cam, go through the door!"

Cam yells back, "I have a plan. You jump through; I'll be right behind you."

Hunter nods, then jumps through the door. Landing on his face, Hunter rolls over just in time to see Cam wave to him before slamming the door closed.

Jax asks Hunter, "Where's Cam? He didn't come through."

Hunter stands up, brushing himself off. "He told me to jump

through, and he would follow. When I turned around, I could see Jim and Hangman approaching him as he waved to me and then slammed the door shut."

Bug yells, "They'll release him!"

Spin Doll replies, "He released himself to save us. He knew he wasn't long for his world, so he gave us a chance to return Bee by sacrificing himself."

Hunter gestures for the group to exit the cave. Once outside, Hunter has them all stand back as he goes back into the cave for something that will burn. Finding a liquid substance that has a no-heat sign on it, Hunter pours it all over each door then places a piece of metal on the floor in front of the first door. Next, he finds a rope. Starting at the first door, he goes from door to door, laying the rope on the ground. Once finished, he ties the end of the rope to the piece of metal that lies in front of the first door.

Hunter walks to the cave's exit, pulls his stick out and cocks it. He aims at the piece of metal and whispers, "Cam, my friend, this one's for you."

Hunter fires a shot at the metal, making it spark. The spark sends the doors ablaze, throwing Hunter from the cave. Bug runs over to help Hunter up and check to make sure his friend is in one piece. Smoke pours out from every exit it can find. Hunter gathers himself and leads the group toward the kingdom. Not looking back, they head off into the woods. Out of the smoke-filled doorway steps an ash-covered Jim and a smoking Hangman.

Jim looks toward the smoking Hangman. "I'm hot. They wanted me gone. Now they're about to find out why. Not for nothing, Hangman, but you're on fire."

Jim pats the fire out on his friend as they head down the freshly made path that Hunter and his crew took.

Chapter 17

"A queen must protect all she rules over." –Dayne

After about a fifteen-minute walk, Willow leads the queen to a dirt road then whistles as a thunderous noise comes racing toward the group. Stopping directly in front of each knight is a purple unicorn draped in golden armor. Willow assists the queen onto his unicorn, and Russell helps Dak upon his. Once all are mounted, Willow gives the signal, and they trot off. The unicorns pick up speed until they are at full running mode. The wind blows Dayne's hair back as she tries to catch her breath. Racing at a speed much faster than a normal horse could reach, Dak watches the ground pass under his feet in a blur. The quick motion makes Dak feel ill, as he pukes across the blurring ground. After over an hour of riding, the unicorns begin to slow their pace to a gallop. Soon, they come to a halt.

"Why are we stopping here?"

Willow raises his finger to his mouth to encourage everyone to be quiet. Silently, they all sit and listen, while the unicorns begin to get fidgety.

Color begins to return to Dak's face. Now feeling a little better, he whispers, "What are we doing?"

"Listening," Willow says.

"Listening to what?"

"Listening for Ones. That's what we listen for."

"Okay, I'll ask—what are Ones?" Dak asks with an eye roll.

"Ones are giant creatures with only one eye," Chet adds.

"So, they're cyclops," Dak implies.

"Kind of, but these are big. What's weird is that they have very poor eyesight. If they hear you or smell you, you're in a lot of trouble," Chet finishes.

Dak swallows hard. "Will they eat us?"

The knights all laugh. "Most definitely, but the worst thing is that they treat you as if you are a toy first. I heard of one person who was used to clean a backside." They laugh again. "Boy, that's a shitty way to lose your light."

Dak is not laughing. "Where are they? I don't see any one-eyed monsters."

Willow once again presses his fingers to his lips and whispers, "Down in that valley among all those purple and teal flowers. They guard the Never Lights."

Dayne gazes out and sees the valley of flowers she and Cam crossed. She desperately needs to go to the field and save the little ones. "Take me to the valley at once; they need me."

"I'm sorry, but it is not safe down there. You, my queen, placed the Ones in the valley. You placed them to protect the Never Lights, and that is what they do."

"They will hurt me, and possibly their queen? Also, they're not baby breaths. They are forget-me-nots."

"I'm sorry, my queen, yes, they are forget-me-nots. I do not think it is safe for you to travel in the valley—not being yourself and all."

"If I truly am your queen, then I demand you take me to the Never Lights immediately!"

"As you wish, my queen," the nights say.

"My queen, I will take you into the valley. The rest can return to Paradise," Mav says, stepping forward.

"Thank you so much, Mav. Now the rest of you return to Paradise. Do not let me find out that one hair on Dak's head was touched. Do I make myself clear?" Dayne warns.

Willow and the rest of the knights agree, and they take Dak and ride off to Paradise.

Mav suggests that the queen leaves her horned steed and ride with him in case they have to get away quickly. Dayne agrees and climbs on the back of Mav's unicorn. Slowly, they trot down the hill toward the valley. The closer they get to the Never Lights, the louder the baby sounds get.

Reaching the edge of the field of flowers, a loud voice echoes toward them. "Stop! Who dares approaches the Never Lights?"

Dayne, not frightened, replies, "It is your queen."

"My queen? My queen is no more. She has left Paradise, never to return. If you don't turn around, imposter, then you will never leave."

Dayne stands firm. "I will not leave! I am who I say I am."

The earth begins to rumble as eleven Ones rise from the dirt ground. As they stand, dirt falls from their massive frames.

Amazed, Dayne whispers, "Mav, they live in the ground?"

"No, they can sleep for a long time. If they aren't disturbed, the flowers cover them so they cannot be snuck up on."

The biggest of the Ones speaks. "You do not smell like our queen. Imposter, I will give you one last time to leave."

Dayne yells back as dirt continues to fall from the giants. "Who else would approach the mighty Ones? I am the Queen of Paradise, and you will address me as such."

Mav turns the unicorn in the opposite direction in case the Ones do not believe her. The Ones place their noses in the air. Still not smelling the familiar smell of the queen, they begin to step toward the pair. Wasting no time, Mav kicks the sides of the steed. The unicorn bursts out running, as the Ones begin to chase. Even though the unicorn is built for speed, the thunderous steps are getting closer. Soon, the giant Shadows of the Ones engulf the pair. They are losing ground with every step. Once they reach the top of the valley, the thunderous sounds end.

"Where did they go?" Dayne questions.

Mav turns the steed back toward the edge of the valley ridge. "They must have stopped at the edge of the valley. Maybe they can't leave the valley."

Mav jumps off the unicorn to look over the edge. Upon reaching the edge, Mav turns and sprints back toward Dayne. A giant hand rises over top of him, as he dives to the side.

The giant hand crashes to the ground, just missing Mav. The One's big eye rises from the edge. "Oh, there you are, imposter."

Before Dayne can react, the One scoops her and the unicorn up in his hand. Dayne pulls the releaser out and gets into her fighting stance. The giant One tosses the unicorn into the air and swallows it with one gulp.

"How dare you treat your queen in this manner?" Dayne stands firm.

"If you are truly my queen, then you will know these three answers to my questions."

Dayne, not knowing if she will know the answers, yells back, "And if I know these answers, you will free me and my friend! Then you will let me tend to the children."

"Agreed, but if you are wrong, you and your friend will join your unicorn."

The One begins with the first question. "Where are the stars?"

Dayne looks at the sky, hoping the stories she was told are true. "They were pulled from the sky. Evil used them to entrap the good. It is my job to return them, and I can't do that with you holding me here. So, now, you are keeping them down here."

The One thinks for a moment as Dayne and Mav wait for his decision.

Satisfied with the answer given, the One begins with the second question, tightening its grip. "My queen has always traveled with a dragon. I see no dragon with you. Where is it?"

"My dragon is here with me. If you release your grip a little, I will show you."

The One opens his hand slightly, and Dayne reaches into her bag and pulls out the chest. She opens it to reveal the beautiful dragon egg.

The One turns his head away from it, because the shine from the egg is even too bright for his poor sight.

"What is that awful light?" he bellows.

"It is a dragon's egg. Soon it will hatch, and my dragon will once again be by my side!" Dayne shouts back.

"Alright, alright, put it away. You've answered the second one."

Dayne closes the chest and returns it to her bag. Mav, impressed with his queen's answers, fears the third question due to the One not being happy about losing.

The One, also surprised, thinks for a minute, deciding on what question only the queen would know. The final question is asked with a smug look on his face. "Okay, my queen, if that's what you are. What are the Never Lights?"

Dayne thinks for a moment and finally answers when the One tightens his grip. "The Never Lights are the babies who were never born. The babies and young children who had no choice in their demise. They never felt the true love of a mother and father. They are lost in a field of their peers, wanting and needing to be held and told it'll be alright. They need to be needed, loved, and taken care of. I walk the field and save them one at a time. It's my job to make sure each and every one of them makes it inside the Paradise gate. I placed you here to watch over them while the Horizon was in chaos. So that's my answer. Now free us this minute."

The One stands silently, dazed, thinking of Dayne's answer. Dayne looks questioningly at Mav, then, without any other words, the One falls to one knee and places Dayne and Mav safely on the ground and gestures Dayne toward the field of Never Lights.

Chapter 18

"The battle becomes easier when friends have your back." –Cam

With Hunter and the group farther up ahead of Jim and a still-smoking Hangman, Jim pulls a small disc resembling a poker chip from his pocket and holds it up to show Hangman.

"After this one, I only have three fast forwards left. So, if you don't mind the walk, I'll see you at the kingdom."

Jim tosses the chip on the ground and proceeds to step on it. The chip sucks him in, and he disappears, leaving Hangman standing alone.

Jim reappears in front of the kingdom gates. He does the dance routine, then enters the gates.

In the meantime, Hangman follows Hunter's path. With smoke billowing out of every crack of the cave, another shadow of a person appears in the cave door.

The smoke-covered figure speaks. "If the evil wants to dance, then who am I to pass on a dance partner?"

Hunter and the group decide to take a quick break, mainly because the baby is hungry. They find a clearing with a nice big fallen log to sit and rest on. Spin Doll pulls out one of the cans of peaches she found on the store floor. She opens it, and the baby begins to eat.

Curiously, Bug asks, "What do you think is so special about this baby? Why would an old guy like Jim search both worlds for him?"

Hunter says, "No idea, but the baby definitely must be special."

"When I touched the baby back in our world, it made me watch myself explode during the war."

"Really? I mean, that is the way you lost your light here," Hunter says.

Bug turns and looks at Hunter. "I blew up!"

"You did, but you did it to save all your friends' lives. That, and because you ate all three pieces of the glass heart," Hunter informs Bug with a laugh.

"If you are done talking war stories, the baby has finished," Spin Doll interrupts.

Jax stands. "Then what are we waiting for? Let's go. Besides, this place is creepy."

They all stand, then proceed toward the kingdom.

Not long after they leave, Hangman arrives at their resting place. Noticing the empty can of peaches, he picks it up, only to crush it in his hands. He tosses it to the ground behind him and begins to walk away.

A voice from behind surprises Hangman.

"Now, littering will not be tolerated. I suggest you pick it up."

The Hangman looks around but sees no one. He turns back to walk away.

"Maybe you didn't hear me correctly. I said pick it up!" the voice shouts as it bounces the crushed can off the back of Hangman's head.

Angrily, Hangman spins around and sees Cam. But this isn't like the sick, feeble Cam they left back at the last world. No, this Cam is ripped and healthy.

He says in a serious tone, "Pick up the can or I'll make you pick it up. Either way, you will remove the trash."

"Boy! You definitely don't want this smoke. I'm not the one to play with. I'll strip you of your light and leave what's left as a reminder to the rest of the Horizon."

Cam dances from side to side, singing, "Who's afraid of the big bad wolf, the big bad wolf?"

The Hangman swings at Cam, but Cam is too quick for the slow swing.

Laughing, Cam says, "Hangman, let me introduce myself. My name is Axel to you. To the rest of the world, it's Cam. Axel is what you will call me; it sounds much tougher than Cam. Besides, you don't want the Horizon to know you got destroyed by a guy named Cam. I mean, you can't walk into a bar and tell people you got beaten up by a guy named Cam. Now you tell them Axel beat your ass, they'll give you a little more respect."

The Hangman swings twice more, missing just as he did with first. Frustrated, he grumbles, "Axel is a fitting name, since I'm going to leave you into a puddle of grease, boy."

The Hangman continues to swing as Cam continues to avoid them. They are accomplishing nothing but tiring themselves out. Finally, both stop, too exhausted to continue.

While breathing heavy, Cam announces, "I think it's my turn on offence."

The Hangman laughs. "Go ahead; whatever hurts me makes me stronger." The Hangman holds his arms up, offering Cam a free shot.

Cam insists that Hangman close his eyes so he doesn't flinch, and this makes Hangman chuckle but he agrees. With eyes closed, Hangman can't see a giant shadow appear from behind.

Cam says, "Here it comes, ugly."

Hangman raises his chin to taunt Cam. The shadow grows bigger as it approaches, and Cam steps back away from Hangman. Eyes widening, Cam stares over top of the big unexpecting man. The shadow stops, and Cam yells, "Hangman, let me introduce you to my friend, Char!"

A loud screech from Char fills the Horizon and startles Hangman, who opens his eyes and turns. The large dragon hovers above Hangman, and before he can react, Char removes his head with her powerful jaws.

As Hangman falls to the ground, Char viciously tears his arms and legs from his body then gathers the parts and flies off with an even louder screech, leaving Cam standing in awe of what he had just witnessed his friend do. Then, having no idea where his friend flew off with Hangman, he starts running to try and catch up with Hunter and the crew.

* * *

Hunter and Bug stop in their tracks, and a shiver runs up Bug's back from the hideous screech. He whispers, "Did that screech sound familiar to you? I feel as if we've heard that before."

Hunter laughs. "It sounded like the first time you were face-to-face with Char. You know, when you shit your pants. You're so nasty."

Bug turns to Spin Doll and Jax and refutes, "I've never shit my pants. Don't listen to a word he says. For all we know, he shit his pants."

Hunter shakes his head and mutters, "You're so nasty. Did you just shit them again? I'm sure I smell something."

Bug punches him. "I did not shit my pants!"

As they start to walk, they notice Bug sniffing the air and subtly checking himself.

Chapter 19

"I believe everyone has a little evil in them. It's weather they let it out or not." –Cam

Jim walks in on the three kings, celebrating and drinking wine. Not amused, he states, "Well, it's nice to see you all celebrating. I'd join you, but it seems I'm busy trying to clear up our baby problem."

Furrow flings back, "Oh, really, the war is over. We won."

Jim shakes his head in disgust. "You won? Ha! What did you win? The baby is on its way here. That doesn't seem like a win to me."

Truncheon whispers under his breath, "I see Hunter didn't live up to his hype."

Jim clamors back, "What didn't Hunter live up to?" Jim looks at each king one at a time as the kings look away from him. Then it hits him. "Did you guys send Hunter after me?"

Paragon jokes, "If we did, he didn't follow orders."

Jim shakes his head. "You dirty bastards. I set up this big lie so you can all sit on a throne and do nothing. This is how you repay me—by sending Hunter after me. Let me tell you something, you worthless scum. When Hunter and Dax find out the truth, you'll all be released. I'll just sit back and watch."

Furrow narrows his eyes. "The King of Evil is no more, and the first lady king is missing. Hopefully, she stumbles upon the same fate as her husband, the dark marked angel. Dak will be fed to Octoro's babies. Hunter and Bug Boy will be sent to the hole for disobeying orders. Now the baby, this one's special. Once the storyteller is no more, our story can never change."

All three kings laugh out loud.

"Fools!" Jim shouts. "You are all a bunch of fools! If the so-called lady king reaches Paradise, you'll need that baby. I'm sure her seven swords are looking for her as we speak. Another thing, where are the Jokers?"

Paragon, leaning back as he takes a seat, replies, "Who needs the weird Jokers? It'd be the best thing for everyone if they got lost and never returned. Now, let's explain how this is going to work. Release Dak when he returns, throw Bug and Hunter in the hole, relieve the lady king of her position, and you find a little piece of the Horizon way back in the corner and never show your face again. Oh yeah, and the baby will be released on sight."

Jim is flabbergasted. "Idiots! If the lady king reaches her pearl gates and reunites with the seven swords, they will come for us. As far as releasing the baby on sight, if you do this, you will release everyone trapped in star orbs. This will send all the stars back to the sky, leaving the tormented souls free. The king of evil will once again walk among us."

Truncheon laughs. "Where is your mindless bodyguard? You dare approach us without him?"

The three kings pull their swords as they surround Jim.

Hunter's voice is suddenly heard behind them. "These are my kings. Three mighty kings, trying to release one old guy. Where is Dayne? We need to speak to her immediately."

Furrow screams, "How dare you talk to your kings in that tone! We sent you to release Jim and Hangman. Instead, you bring us back a baby. To the hole with these three!"

Bug turns to Hunter. "I thought you said these were the good guys."

Hunter shrugs, and Bug faces the kings. "Well, let me explain why we won't be going into the hole." Then, looking at Hunter once more, he says, "Well, partner, are you ready to dance?"

Hunter smiles. "Time to make you guys a memory."

Hunter and Bug draw their weapons. Spin Doll and Jax take Baby Bee and run off. The kings, feeling good about their odds, move closer to Hunter and Bug.

Furrow blurts, "Well, it's four on two. I really like the odds."

Jim backs away. "You mean three on two. Don't count me in this fight."

Paragon yells, "You coward! Run with your tail between your legs. We'll settle our issue later."

Another voice joins. "I think it's three on three. At least, that's my count."

Cam appears beside Bug and Hunter, holding a new, shiny sword. Hunter and Bug can't believe their eyes as a buff Cam stands next to them.

Bug says, "What the hell happened to you?"

Cam smiles. "I'll tell you the whole story once we get done mopping up these fakes."

The kings circle the three warriors. But before they attack, Furrow yells to the angels for backup. Twenty or so angels fall in behind the kings. Paragon yells, "Did you really think you could challenge your kings and win?"

Bug counters, "That's why you play the game. Trust me, not all underdogs lose. But, since we're here, we'll bat first."

Bug swings his bat, hitting Truncheon in the head and sending him to the ground. The crowd of onlookers fall silent. No one can believe Bug hit a king. Bug turns to Hunter, smiling. "You're up next. Make it count."

Paragon demands the angels attack the traitors. The angels attack with full force, but the warriors are too much for them. The kings send for more angels. Cam suggests the three retreat instead of releasing even more angels. Hunter and Bug agree as they make a run for it. Only releasing the angels they have to, they quickly exit the kingdom.

Chapter 20

"Never trust two tongues against one." –Willow

The remaining six knights and Dak come upon a beautiful golden wall that seems to go on forever.

Dak curiously asks, "What is this?"

Willow answers, "It is the wall between here and Paradise."

Dak, amazed at the glimmering wall, stands wide-eyed. "May I touch it?"

Russell replies, "You may, but I'm sure the Paradise military will come calling soon after the touching."

"Aren't *you* military?"

Megan shakes her head. "We are the seven swords. We protect the queen and anyone who travels there. The military guards the Paradise wall and all who live within."

Russell adds, "We freely travel in and out of the pearl gates, as the military is prohibited."

"If the military can't exit the gate, how will they stop me from touching the wall?"

Willow laughs and dares Dak. "Go ahead and touch it. I'm up for a good show."

Dak, thinking they're bullshitting him, runs up and puts the bottom of his foot on the wall. The knights amusingly look at each other.

A voice from the top of the wall yells, "Who dares touch the wall of Paradise?"

Dak looks up and sees a soldier with a handlebar mustache looking down at him. "I'm sorry. I didn't know you couldn't touch the wall."

The soldier replies, "Remove your foot, or I'll remove it from your body. I will not ask again."

Dak quickly removes his foot. "I'm really sorry. I promise it'll never happen again."

The soldier counters, "See that it doesn't." Then he disappears behind the wall.

The knights laugh out loud.

Russell mocks the soldier. "Remove your foot, or I'll remove it."

Dak asks, "Why are you laughing? He seemed really mad."

Willow stops laughing. "Because he looks big on top of that wall. But, down at ground level, he's only three-and-a-half feet tall."

"He's a midget?"

Megan stops laughing. "Please don't ever call him a midget. He is a dwarf, and a very touchy dwarf. Dwarfs are extremely powerful. They can lift two times their weight."

Willow adds, "I once saw a dwarf lift a horse and cart together over his head."

Megan nods. "Oh yeah. I once saw a dwarf carry three full-size logs at once while eating an apple."

Russell starts laughing. "That's nothing. I once saw a dwarf carry Willow's mom to the buffet, and, even more impressively, he carried her back to her table."

Everyone goes eerily quiet. Then, all at once, they burst out laughing. Dak can't believe how different the knights act out of sight of the queen. Suddenly, their laughter stops as they notice some people approaching.

Willow yells, "Stop! Who goes there?"

One of the intruders yells back. "We're friends; we mean no harm."

The closer they get; the knights can tell there are three of them.

Willow yells at them once again. "Stop, or we'll be forced to pull our swords!"

Now much closer, Dak can see it's the Jokers and their sister. Dak demands the knights untie his hands.

"You must untie me. Those are not friends. They are the ones who caused all the chaos in my kingdom. They are very bad people."

About twenty feet apart, Willow orders, "Stop, that will be close enough. My friend here tells me you are not good people."

Sin responds, "Or maybe it is *he* that is not good."

The knights look at Dak.

Willow asks, "What makes you better than them?"

Dak, surprised when the knights ask him that question, answers, "My mother is your queen. Also, I did not resist being tied up. Justice will always prove your worth."

Omin interrupts. "Who's Justice? We seem to be on opposite sides, but who can say their side is better than the other?"

Russell steps in. "Whether good or bad, why do you two guys have the word clown tattooed on your forehead?"

Dak snickers. "My mom, your queen, had that written on their foreheads."

Willow is puzzled. "Did it hurt? I didn't realize you two were clowns; you look more like a couple of Jokers."

Cozzex answers for her brothers. "They *are* Jokers. This guy's mom thought it would be funny to make my brothers walk around with that on their heads as a punishment."

Russell replies to Cozzex, "My lady, forgive me. Until you spoke, I had no idea you were a lady. I truly feel almost as dumb as your brothers look."

Chet adds, "Now, Russell, that was a mean thing to say. Maybe they are all ladies."

Sin stops him. "We are not ladies!"

Russell smirks. "Okay, okay, let's not make the clowns mad. Clowns are supposed to be happy."

Sin and Omin are hopping mad, but they know they stand no chance against the seven swords.

Dak queries, "If they're so good, then why did they release my father?"

Cozzex answers, "Your father was the bad guy. He led the attack on our peaceful farm. He destroyed our hard-working factory. Or, what about your father destroying the good witch's house—for no reason? He didn't even know you were his son. That, my knights, does not sound like a good guy."

The knights shake their heads up and down, almost agreeing with Cozzex.

The bickering worsens between Dak and the Jokers until Willow decides to also tie up the Jokers. He explains, "We will keep the marked angel and the Jokers bound and gagged till the queen returns. She can then decide the fate of these four. The rest of us will set up camp for the night. Hopefully, the queen will return by morning's light."

Camp is quickly built, and everyone is soon asleep. All but Russell, who draws night watch.

Chapter 21

"When being bad looks so good, you can rule the Horizon." –Dak

Mav follows behind Dayne as they walk down the hillside to the fields of Never Lights. Each giant One they walk past kneels and says, "My queen." Once they reach the bottom, they stand at the edge of the field. Mav is astonished when he perceives the sound of infants chirping. Turning to ask Dayne if she could hear them as well, he notices her eyes are filled with tears. She bends over and takes the first flower in her hands. Mav stands there and listens.

Dayne begins to speak to the flower. "My precious little one. You had so much love to give. You were ready for the world, but the world wasn't ready for you. The love you seek, I will hand to you inside the Paradise walls. Someday, your mother and father will hold you tight to their hearts and hands."

Mav is shocked and awed as he watches the flower turn into a beautiful baby girl. Her smile is so innocent, it breaks his heart in two. Dayne turns toward the One and places the baby girl in his giant hand. When she doesn't cry, Mav is sure she feels safe.

Dayne then turns to the next flower. As she caresses it, she says, "Oh my, what a handsome little guy. Your world accepted you for such a short time. You have your father's smile and your mother's heart. If only given a chance, you would've changed your world." She turns and places the little boy beside the sleeping girl in the giant's hands. Mav watches as baby after baby is placed in his hands.

Finally, the largest One addresses the queen. "My queen, our hands are full. We must deliver them to Paradise. I'm sorry, but we must leave the rest for now."

Without raising her voice, the queen replies to the One's request, "I will not leave these children. Please take these to Paradise. When you arrive, ask for Owl. He will accept each child into Paradise, then you will return here for the rest. I will wait beside them till your return. If you see my knights, ask them to join us."

The One answers, "Yes, my queen. But there will be many trips to return every baby to Paradise."

Dayne turns away from the One. "Then let's not waste time standing around talking. Please be on your way."

The Ones begin to climb the valley wall as each one carries hands full of babies toward Paradise. Dayne walks back to the edge of the flowers to assure them they won't be alone again. Mav joins her as he carefully talks to the flowers.

With giant steps, the Ones are much quicker than the knights reaching Paradise. The knights watch as each giant walks past their makeshift camp. The One approaches the gate of pearls, still holding his hands out.

At the top of the wall, a very small man appears. "May I help you, sir?"

The One pushes his hand toward the small man. "A gift for you from the queen."

The small man barks, "What do you mean, a gift?"

"My queen said to hand the babies to the gatekeeper named Owl."

Upon hearing this, Owl immediately opens the gate. Once all the babies are removed from the One's hands, Owl asks, "Is that all, or would you like something else?"

The One turns and looks to the side of the wall. Owl looks to see what the One is looking at. This, in turn, reveals a line of Ones all holding handfuls of babies.

Owl yells, "Next!" as the next one approaches.

The finished One approaches the knights. Looking down at them all, he informs them, "My queen has ordered every one of you to help her at the Never Light field."

Willow stands and responds, "We're not all knights here. Four of us are prisoners."

The One leans toward Willow. "The queen said *all*. So, *all* will be going." The One stands back up and heads for the valley once again.

Russell yells, "Well, boys and girls, it looks like we're all on babysitting duties!"

The knights order the Jokers and Dak to walk ahead of them. Unwillingly, the Jokers walk beside Dak while the knights walk closely behind.

Dak whispers to the Jokers, "Before the day is over, I will release you all."

Sin snickers. "Watch your mouth, boy, or you might end up like your pops."

Anger fills Dak and he turns to Sin, slamming his face into Sin's face.

Dak screams, "I will release you, clown!"

Sin screams back while a small cut opens on his forehead and begins to trickle blood down his face. "If they untied these ropes, I would end you, boy!"

Dak instantly turns to Willow. "Please untie these ropes. After I release these clowns, I promise you can tie me back up."

Sin requests the same.

Hesitantly, Willow unties them both. The knights circle the two, as they are just as excited to see a good fight. Dak swings first, landing a punch on Sin's face, sending him to the ground. Sin reacts by grabbing a handful of dirt and throwing it in Dak's eyes. Dak stumbles backward as he tries to wipe the dirt from his eyes. Taking advantage of having the upper hand, Sin tackles Dak to the ground. Rolling around on the ground, each fighter gets in a couple of good shots. Dak gets to his feet first and notices his releaser on one of the unicorns. The unsuspecting knights let him grab his sword from the Beast. Dak holds the releaser toward Sin's face and growls, "Any last words, clown?"

Sin looks toward Willow and begs, "My sword, can I please have it? If I'm to be released today, let me be released with dignity."

Russell tosses Sin his sword. "Everyone deserves a fighting chance."

Dak and Sin circle each other, waiting for the other to make the first mistake. The cheering knights pay no attention to Cozzex and Omin, who are slowly picking up their swords. Dak and Sin collide with swords a couple of times, with neither gaining the upper hand. Slowly, they work themselves closer to Willow, drawing back their swords, ready to swing for the final blow.

Cozzex and Omin quickly grab a hostage, placing swords to their necks.

Willow steps between Dak and Sin, stopping the fight, and yells, "Let them go or be released yourself!"

Dak and Sin draw their swords to each side of Willow's head. Chet and Larry drew their swords.

Sin says, "I'd place your weapons on the ground in front of you, or Willow here will no longer be with us for the rest of this discussion."

Willow drops his sword to the ground as the rest of the knights in turn join him. Omin sets Russell free, then orders him to pick up the knights' weapons and place them on one unicorn. Russell follows Omin's orders and loads the weapons onto his steed.

Omin says, "Now, if you'd be so kind as to all sit with your backs to each other."

Sin adds, "So, pick a partner, please."

Willow, in a low tone, threatens, "You know you all will be released for this."

Sin finishes tying Willow's hands and pats him on the back "We all get released eventually. I just know today is not that day."

With all the knights tied and sitting with their backs to each other, Cozzex yells, "Girls, you can come out now!"

Mimic flies out from behind an old stone wall. They rush to Dak and excitedly yell, "Dak, you're alive!"

Dak smiles. "Yes, girls, I'm alive, and I'd like to keep it that way."

As they hug, Dak whispers something to the girls, who then fly over to the unicorn with all the weapons. Each one grabs one side of the reins, and, with a sharp "Ya!" the unicorn takes off running. Then Sin, Omin, Cozzex, and Dak mount a unicorn, leaving one standing alone. Dak trots over to the lone unicorn, bends down, and slaps it one the ass. The unicorn takes off through the woods.

Dak rides in front of the bound and gagged knights and says, "If it weren't for the queen being my mother, she would no longer be with us. My father was the Dark King. But thanks to my friends here, he's gone, and now I'll be the new Dark King. Willow, you were right about me being the marked angel. But you missed one thing." Dak pulls his shirt off, revealing the mark. "It's a mark, alright. But it's a dark mark. So, I'm the Dark Angel King, but you can call me Dak."

Sin's mouth falls open. "No shit. Never even thought of that. That's why you're named Dak."

Willow spits his gag out and yells, "Dark Angel King, you will perish to my blade! This, I guarantee to you."

Dak smiles. "That's nice to know. But I think I'll be leaving now. I have a kingdom to command. Oh, if I were you guys, I'd try to escape as soon as possible. With the big creatures carrying the Never Lights back and forth to Paradise, I'd be worried I'd get stepped on. Russell, I don't think you'd look good flat."

Dak points toward the kingdom as they race off to it.

Russell looks at Willow and says, "Dark Angel King my ass. Next time we meet up with him, he'll be the Dead Ass King."

Willow agrees. "Yes, but at this moment, we need to free ourselves quickly."

Suddenly, a thunderous noise and rumbling ground means only one thing.

The Ones are returning.

Chapter 22

"It's hard to believe that when evil rears its face, it could be a friend."
–Hunter

Spin Doll and Jax slow their pace as they found a nice spot secluded by hanging limbs. They stop to rest and wait for the men to return from the kingdom. In the meantime, hopefully find some friendlies. After making sure Bee is fed, Spin Doll and Jax eat a handful of berries they find. Spin Doll watches as Bee stumbles around chasing a butterfly who wants to play tag. This brings a smile to Spin Doll's face.

Jax sits impatiently, wanting to ask Spin Doll a question. Sensing this, Spin Doll asks, "Something on your mind, Jax?"

Jax shakes her head, even though Spin Doll can tell something is bugging her.

Spin Doll attempts again. "Are you sure, because it looks like something is puzzling you?"

Jax gives in and explains, "If the kings are good, then why were they so mean? We brought them the baby, like you said they wanted. I saw this earlier when Bee touched me on our walk here." She shakes her head and continues. "When I think of the Horizon, I think of sunsets and beautiful days, smiles, and no more pain. I thought everyone would be happy and get along. But, as soon as we arrived, I saw unhappy, mean people. That seemed to fill the air. If this is our last stop, it should welcome us, not threaten us. Why isn't there a place with no hate?"

Tears begin to trickle down Jax's face. Spin Doll gets up and moves over to her and gives Jax a big hug, which brings the tears quicker. Baby Bee stumbles over and places his hand on Jax's knee. Jax's mind instantly sees a beautiful world filled with smiles and happiness. Children play hopscotch and merry-go-round. This is the place Jax thought of when she heard they were going to the Horizon. Baby Bee removes his hand and goes back to playing tag with the butterfly.

Jax wipes her eyes. "I saw what the Horizon should be. We need to rid this place of evil."

Spin Doll releases her hug and says, "We will, Jax. We will. Once we get all the warriors together, we'll go pay the kings a visit."

"There you are. We've searched for over an hour," Hunter says, suddenly appearing.

Bug walks over to Spin Doll and sits beside her. "Are you two alright?"

The girls nod, and Spin Doll says, "What was that? Why'd the kings seem different?"

Hunter answers, "Maybe they're not the kings we thought they were. Maybe it's not good to be the kings."

Bug blurts out, "Now that they messed with thunder and lightning, they just made a bigger problem."

Hunter laughs. "Let me guess, you're thunder."

Bug shakes his head. "Oh, by the way, Spin Doll, your baby is eating a butterfly."

Spin Doll quickly jumps up and wipes the mangled butterfly from Bee's mouth.

Hunter stands, looking out between the branches. "Well, since heading back to the kingdom sounds like more trouble than it's worth, I guess we go in the opposite direction. Anyone up for some exploring?"

"Oh, most definitely, Hunter. Count me in," Cam states as he appears.

Bug rolls his eyes. "Okay, Cam. Who's your supplier for steroids? Because you look like a before and after picture."

Hunter furrows his brows. "Yeah, what gives? When I last saw you, you were sacrificing yourself for us. Now it looks as if you're ready for a bodybuilding competition."

Cam grins. "When I slammed that door shut, I disappeared. The Hangman and Jim went high, and I went low, then belly crawled away from them. Not finding me, they entered the door with Jim's key. But before the door slammed shut, I blocked it with my foot. With the cave filled with smoke, they never noticed me. I saw them exit the cave; as a matter of fact, I think Hangman was on fire. I waited in the smoke-filled cave till they left to find you. Then, with the disease and hard breathing, I collapsed out of the cave's entrance. Then I woke up all jacked and felt great. I rolled over to see Char staring back at me. Knowing I wasn't long for this world, she acted fast. She poked the middle of her hand, making it bleed, then squeezed her bloody hand and made drops of blood fall into my mouth. Instantly, I felt new. No more pain, coughing, or weakness, and my strength grew four times right there! My sickness was overthrown by Char's blood. It may sound stupid, but I believe everyone receives one miracle. That, my friends, was my miracle."

Bug sighs. "Really, one miracle. What about being brought here to try and release you from your pain? Or how about Colt giving up her light to give you a life you never had? Now Char gives you one more chance. To me, that's three miracles. If you only get one, then you just used two that weren't yours!"

Cam frowns. "My first light was turned off by defeating the witch. My second light was turned off by defeating Octoro. My third one may start by kicking your ass, you ungrateful worm."

Bug pulls at his bat as he and Cam walk toward each other.

Hunter jumps in between the two, and Jax covers her ears. Tears begin to roll down her face as she watches the two friends try to get at each other. Finally, she can't take it anymore.

"Stop it! Stop it! What is wrong with everyone in both worlds? Why can't we never escape hate? Our lives are so bad, we must blame everyone but ourselves. Who cares how Cam got here? Just be happy that he's here with us. If Colt surrendered her light for him, and Char gave him her blood, obviously they think he's good, so who cares? I wanna be happy that you're all here with me. Why do you make it so hard?"

Jax covers her head with her arms and continues to cry. Baby Bee stumbles to her once again and puts his head on her leg, trying to comfort her. Hunter gives Cam and Bug each a shove in opposite directions.

Spin Doll begins to speak but is interrupted by Dak riding in on a unicorn.

"My friends, what's all the commotion?"

Jax never looks up, but Spin Doll jumps to her feet. She squeals, "Dak, where have you been? Your mother is missing, and the kings are changed for the worse."

Dak, acting as if he knows nothing about his mom, asks, "What about my mother? You said she's missing. How long has she been gone, and which way did she leave?"

Bug laughs. "Nice unicorn, Daisy."

Dak hops off the unicorn and ignores Bug as he walks by him. Cam steps back and disappears, realizing Dak hasn't noticed him.

Dak says, "Who do we have here?" He stands in front of Jax, waiting for her to look up at him.

Spin Doll answers for her. "This is Jax. She helped save—"

Dak interrupts her. "Is that a baby here in the Horizon?"

Hunter picks up Baby Bee before Dak can reach him. "This strong little man is Bee."

Dak gestures to hold Bee. "What a precious little man. Can I hold him?"

Spin Doll shouts, "No! Don't touch him. He's got the ability to tell you your past or future just by touching you."

Dak walks over to the child, wanting to see for himself. Bee reaches up and touches Dak's face. Instantly, Dak has a vision of standing in a pile of bricks and rubbish. Fire burns in little spots randomly around him. He stands alone, smiling. Bee pulls his hand away and buries his face in Hunter's chest.

Dak's eyes widened with excitement. He turns to Spin Doll and asks, "Is this the child they call the storyteller?"

"Yes, but he shies away from evil… kind of like he just did you."

Hunter pulls out his stick with the use of one hand, still holding Bee with the other one. Bug and Spin Doll pull their weapons as well.

Dak chuckles. "What are you guys thinking? I'm not a bad guy. I was with you at the barn, factory, and the war on the hill. I led the humans in that battle. You guys know my mom and my dad. The only thing I've ever hurt were some blackberries."

Everyone puts their weapons away.

Bug remarks, "Wow, I can't believe for a moment we thought you were bad." Everyone starts laughing except Jax.

Dak adds, "I'm definitely not bad… or at least, I wasn't."

Before he can continue, Sin, Omin, and Cozzex step out from the trees.

Dak looks at Hunter. "The child, please."

Hunter pulls back, refusing to hand over Bee.

Sin speaks. "Oh goodie, he's going to make it the hard way."

Spin Doll rushes Dak, but Dak covers his face with his hand and pushes her to the ground.

"Soon I will be king of the kingdom. I will rule all. They will bow at my feet. I mean, I should've been king. Not my dead-beat dad or my 'save everyone' mom. First lady king, my ass. That throne was mine, and we all know it. Now, I'm just going to take it. I definitely don't need some crying baby trying to stop me. No baby, no story. Besides, most stories are gossip and untruths. So now, are you giving me the baby, or do I have to release you all and then take him?"

Bug yells, "Where's Hoss? There's no way he'd let you do this."

Dak smiles. "Hoss is no longer with us. You see, for a great big man, he was kind of weak."

Hunter disgustedly huffs, "Hoss, weak!"

Dak turns to Hunter. "Let me tell you a little secret about Hoss. You see, Hoss and I were out cleaning up the remaining Shadows, when we stumbled upon a group of twenty or so Shadows. Hoss met them at almost the exact spot Dillo lost his light. Hoss yelled for me to stand behind him so I wouldn't get hurt. Just as the Shadows approached him, I ran my sword through his back. It was hard to push my sword that deep. When I pulled it out, he collapsed to the ground. I never turned back as I walked away. The only sound I heard was the stabbing sounds coming from the Shadows' weapons."

Everyone is stunned to hear Dak's confession.

Bug softly says, "You released Hoss's light?"

Dak whispers back, "You bet your ass I did. I couldn't have that monster ruin my plans."

Spin Doll screams, "You're the monster!"

Dak giggles and says, "Oh, you really don't know how much truth you just told."

Then Dak turns back toward Hunter. "And now the baby, please."

Chapter 23

"Sometimes old memories save us." –Russell

Char disperses Hangman throughout the Horizon. She takes his head to the cave of Never End, while his left arm she drops on the beaches of Seclusion. The Hangman's right arm is planted at the old man and woman's homestead farm. His legs are sent floating down Clear Tears Creek. Finally, Char places his torso and beating heart at the top of Moon Level Mountain, knowing that if Hangman's parts never reach each other, he will not return. So, her plan is to detach him and leave him where only a few can travel. She calls her plan "Six ways to Hangman."

Soaring through the sky on her way back to Cam, she notices the giant Ones carrying something. They march in a straight line, as if they're focused on only one task. Curious, she flies to the end of the line to see where they're coming from. Reaching the valley of Never Lights, she notices Dayne and immediately drops down to visit her.

Char lands with a thud, which startles Dayne and Mav. Mav pulls his sword out and stands between Char and Dayne.

Dayne, happy to see her old friend, yells, "Char, you're back!"

Mav is surprised that the Beast has a name and that his queen is friends with it. "Back, you infernal Beast. I'll save you, my queen."

Dayne laughs. "No need, Mav. This is my friend, Char. Besides, who are you fooling? She'd kick your ass."

Reluctantly, Mav lowers his sword and steps behind Dayne.

Char, surprised to see Dayne in a dress, asks, "Where are the others? Why are you out here alone? Didn't you see those giant one-eyes?"

Dayne laughs. "Those one-eyes work for me. I'm releasing all the Never Lights, and they are taking them to Paradise for me. This is Mav, one of the seven sword knights."

Char waves. "Pleased to meet you, Mav. Any friend of Dayne's is a friend of mine."

Mav shyly waves back.

Dayne asks Char if she's seen the rest of the knights or Dak. But Char hasn't and has no news of them.

Dayne says, "I have a few more Never Lights to attend to. Can you do me a favor and fly north toward Paradise? Try and find my knights, please. If you do, can you bring Dak to me?"

Char agrees and immediately flies off toward the north. Dayne and Mav go back to the Never Lights.

The six knights frantically struggle to try and free themselves, but it's no use. Their bands are too tight.

Willow, trying to calm the group down, says, "Listen, we need to work together. We cannot untie these ropes by ourselves. We must work together."

Russell blurts, "If we're in the path when the Ones come through, we'll for certain be trampled."

Already realizing this, Willow announces, "We must concentrate to free one of us at a time. Trust me, we will not be released today."

They all scoot around Megan and work on freeing her first. Finally, they break her ropes and she's freed. She quickly begins trying to untie Russell's ropes. But the ropes are too tight. Willow orders her to go find their weapons so she can cut the ropes much quicker. Megan runs out into the brush where they watched the Jokers toss their last weapon. The brush is thick and full of thorns, making it almost impossible to find their weapon.

It isn't long before the ground begins to shake. Willow yells, "Megan, hurry, the Ones are returning!"

The knights huddle as close as they possibly can, trying desperately to make themselves a small target. Soon, the ground shakes even more. They can hear the crushing ground with every step.

Willow orders Megan to stay in the thorns, out of trouble. Meanwhile, he tells the rest of the knights, "Men, it has been an honor to ride with you. Who would've thought that the seven swords would be dismantled by four lowlifes? On any given day, one of us could have defeated those four. Sadly, today was not one of those days. I'm sorry I failed you. I have let down Paradise."

Russell smiles. "Aw, buddy, don't blame yourself. It wasn't like we had any plans. I'll tell you what. I could go for a Starletta and a couple slices of pie right now."

Chet laughs. "Who are you fooling? You'd get a whole pie."

Nene says, "You'd probably ask what was for dessert."

All of them start licking their lips, thinking of pie.

Willow adds, "Remember when you'd come running into your grandma's kitchen after she had just pulled a pie out?"

Chet chuckles. "It would instantly burn the roof of your mouth."

Meme adds, "So you'd run to the fridge and drink the milk—right out of the jug."

Russell says, "Then Gram would slap you in the back of the head for drinking out of the jug."

They all begin to laugh as the thunderous footsteps are upon them. Seeing the giant feet only a few steps away from them, they all close their eyes, waiting for their release. Willow peeks, only to see the giant foot directly above him. He closes his eyes once again.

With a final thunderous stomp, the men give up. They don't feel any pain. As a matter of fact, it feels as if they're floating in the air. The wind blows through their hair. The stomping noise gets further away from them.

Russell whispers, "Boys, are we released?"

Willow answers, "Must be. I feel nothing but a slight breeze."

Char's voice joins them. "Guys, you can open your eyes now."

With their eyes still shut, Russell asks, "Who the hell's voice is that? Willow, I don't think we're alone."

Char says, "Guys, you can open your eyes. You're safe."

All the men open their eyes to see the trees and landscape looking very small.

Russell yells, "Are we angels?"

Nene answers, "Nope, but we are being carried by a dragon."

Russell yells back, "Oh, great! Instead of being crushed by the Ones, we're going to be eaten by a dragon."

It isn't long before they begin descending. Char lands in the Never Light valley where she talked to Dayne. Dropping the knights on the ground, she waits for Dayne to finish. Once all the Never Lights have been transported to Paradise, Dayne and Mav approach Char and the knights. Dayne hugs Char.

"Thank you so much, friend. We surely would've lost this war without them."

Char replies, "Anything for you, my queen."

They hug once again.

Mav quickly unties the five knights. "My queen, we seem to be short a knight."

Willow answers, "Megan was hiding in the thick bramble to avoid the Ones. She must still be there."

Dayne looks at Char and asks, "Would you do me just one more favor?"

Char happily replies, "Sure, hop on, my queen."

Dayne climbs atop Char as she explains, We'll go rescue Megan. You six meet us at the pearl gates."

The two friends fly off into the Horizon as the knights begin their trek back to Paradise.

Chapter 24
Part One

"Love can never be lost… or can it?" –Jim

The three kings are furious with Jim. So much so that they threaten to string him up in the center of the kingdom for all to witness. Having Jim escorted to a dungeon cell, the kings deliberate what to do with him. The soldiers have all they can do to force the old man into a cell. For an old man, he still has a lot of fight left in him. But with the numbers against him, he's finally forced into his new living quarters, and the cell door slams shut, making sure he stays at home.

Searching his new confinement, Jim quickly sees that the wall he shares with the next cell is bowing and about to burst. Jim begins to see small cracks in the wall, which to him means it's about to burst. One of the men who forced him in the cell jokes, "Your wall looks like it's about to burst at the seams."

The rest of them laugh as they quickly exit the dungeon, leaving Jim to fend for himself. Jim is spitting nails mad. He isn't as concerned about the wall, thinking whatever is on the other side doesn't want a piece of him at the moment.

After about an hour of stewing in his cell, he can hear footsteps heading toward him. The footsteps stop in front of his cell door. Suddenly the lock on the door clicks open, and the three kings enter his cell. Before Jim can say anything, Paragon speaks. "Up till now, old man, your plan has worked flawlessly."

Furrow interrupts Paragon as he adds, "But now that Dayne has fled the kingdom and we banished all the remaining warriors from it..."

Truncheon finishes. "Also, since the Dark King, Kannon, has been released and is no longer with us, we really don't feel that there's much of a need to keep you around anymore."

Jim angrily barks back, "What do you mean you no longer have a need for me? Are you fucking kidding me right now? I'm the reason you three are even relevant. I'm the one who made the baby sick and had them believing coming to the Horizon to cure it was the only option. I told them that Paradise would be as safe as the night sky. Once the star had landed and taken the shape of the baby, I kidnapped it. I talked that buffoon, Fat Jack, into stealing some of Paradise's doors. I made the Queen of Paradise, and the king of the kingdom believe only they could save the baby. When the baby went missing and all the stars came down to help find it, I was the one who devised a plan to turn them into Shadows. I personally handpicked the warriors and their watchers that helped put you three beggars into power. I broke the king's throne into four and built four thrones out of it. I'm the one who should oversee you bumbling idiots. Release me at once and give me what I should rightfully have!"

Paragon's only reply is, "You shall hang in the middle of the kingdom at first light."

The three kings leave without another word as Jim grabs the cell window bars and screams, "You three pieces of shit will soon pay for disobeying me!"

Truncheon returns to the door and states, "Looks like this is where your story ends. It's a shame you couldn't find Maggie. We'll be sure to give her our regards if we ever run into her. Now, shut up and enjoy the rest of your night. It is your last, you know."

Chuckling to himself, he walks out of Jim's sight. Before leaving the dungeon, Jim can hear the kings joking.

"Good night, Jim, don't let the bedbugs bite!" Paragon shouts.

Jim begins to frantically searched the cell for a way out, hoping to find a loose brick or a frail bar, but it is futile. The cell is solid, and there's nothing he can do to escape. With no answers, Jim begins to talk to himself.

"Well, old man, this might just be your curtain call. Who would've thought a nobody like you could flip the Horizon upside down?"

Instantly, Jim's eyes catch an intruder. A cricket has entered his cell by crawling under the cell door. Jim, bursting at the seams for any kind of conversation, begins to talk to the cricket.

"Well, hello, sir or madam. My name is Jim. Pleased to make your acquaintance."

He politely waits a minute for the cricket to respond. But not a sound comes from the cricket.

"You know, this isn't a safe place for either of us. Whatever is on the other side of this wall, I'm pretty sure it doesn't want to be friends with either of us."

Still nothing from the cricket. Jim, not one to give up, continues. "How'd I end up here, you're wondering? Well, since we can't go anywhere, pull up a chair and I'll tell you. You see, back in my world I was married to the most beautiful girl. For forty-five years, she made me the luckiest man in the world. It's not too often you get to marry your best friend. Every night, we'd walk around town holding hands. People would walk by us and say things like, 'Isn't that cute, after all these years?' or 'That must be some kind of love.' I couldn't help myself from smiling. I would look forward to our walks; it was the favorite part of my day.

"But our world went from cute to chaos overnight. Our world had gotten a sickness that spread like wildflowers. People were dying from it in enormous numbers. Everyone had to wear a mask in public, and the news told us to avoid going out as much as possible. Plus, at our age, we couldn't take a chance catching it. So, Maggie refused to leave our house. Any errands had to be done by me. This changed our world drastically. No more walks or dinner dates. We sat at home and watched the world go crazy. Crime went up along with food and gas prices. Every day on the news, they would talk about looting and rioting in our streets. This terrified my wife to the extreme of being a prisoner in her own home. She had security cameras and double locks on each door. She even convinced me to buy a pistol for protection, even though I'm not really a gun guy."

"One night, we had lost power while watching TV. Frightened, I sent Maggie up to our bedroom, while I went to check our fuses in the basement. Immediately, she went for my gun and locked the bedroom door. I thought I had the gun locked in my nightstand. But she must've known where I hid the key. The fuses were all good, so it must've been a power failure outside the house. Just my luck. As I was making my way up the basement steps, the candlelight blew out, leaving me to feel my way up the remaining stairs. Once I reached the top, worse luck hit me. The basement door was locked. I tried pounding on it and yelling to Maggie. This must've frightened her even more than she already was. The only thing I could do was bust the door down. After several attempts, I finally broke it open. I must've looked like a mess, with a bruised shoulder and a small cut on my face, which seemed to be bleeding more than it should have. I was in quite a decent amount of pain. Immediately, I headed for the bathroom. After fumbling around the medicine cabinet, I found some gauze and wrapped it around my head, trying to stop the bleeding. I must've been some sight.

"I could hear our bedroom door open and Maggie yell my name. I responded, but she must not have heard me. When I came out of the bathroom, I immediately headed up the stairs. As I walked up the stairs—not too quickly, mind you—I could see Maggie's outline standing at the top. Just before reaching the top, I thought I heard Maggie say, 'Stop!' So, I stopped. Before anything else could happen, the lights came back on. The sight of blood and gauze frightened her so. She shot me three times, sending me tumbling to the bottom of the stairs. I lay there in a lump, unable to move and covered in blood. Realizing what she did, she rushed down the stairs and sat beside me. She tried to stop the bleeding as she continued to apologize. I couldn't speak and had no way of calming her down. All I could do was watch her pull the gun on herself. With one shot, her body lay beside mine. My last few thoughts were wondering how my perfect world could change so quickly."

Chapter 24
Part Two

"Love shouldn't be this hard to find." –Jim

The cricket scuttles about for a moment and then returns as if it wants to hear the rest of Jim's story. Jim pleasantly smiles at his new friend, then continues. "The next thing to happen is I woke up in here. The green grass and blue skies felt so inviting. For a few minutes I laid there watching the clouds go by. Then Maggie's image popped into my head. I sat up, immediately searching for my Maggie. She was nowhere to be found. I walked up and down the hillsides, dirt roads, and grassy fields, calling her name. But I received no answer.

"My search led me to the gates of the kingdom. I pounded on the gates till a soldier opened it to greet me. I explained to him that I was just looking for my wife and meant him no harm. He replied that he was sorry, but I would not be allowed to enter. Then he assured me that my wife would not be in such a place. Closing the gate, he added that I should leave and never come back. I was stunned. How could they not want a nice guy like me? I didn't want to stay. I just wanted to look for Maggie."

The cricket scurries off under the door, but soon it returns to hear the conclusion of Jim's story.

"I was so mad I must've sounded like a freight train coming through the woods. Coming to a clearing, I noticed a large, fat man sitting on a rock, staring at a much larger rock. I approached him with caution, as he seemed not to be all there. 'Hey friend, are you all, right?' I asked him. He nods but didn't speak. I slowly sat down beside him and looked to see what he was looking at. There was a hole in the rock big enough to walk into. The fat man began to speak. 'Name is Jack.

But most people call me Fat Jack. This hole in the rock is the entrance to my home. I'm just wondering if I should invest in a door for it.' I answered, 'Well, brother, if I were you, I would.' A huge smile filled his face, showing off what looked like metal teeth. Before I could do anything, he had me in a bear hug, yelling, 'My brother! I always wanted a brother.' His strength was immense, and I knew immediately I needed him to help me find Maggie.

"While we assembled a door for his rock house, I explained how I lost his sister-in-law and how we need to find her. He explained how he met these two guys that looked like clowns. They were just over the hill, living in an old factory building. Not the friendliest people—maybe even a little scary. Well, that sounded like the kind of people we needed. So, we headed for the brother clowns.

"Reaching the old building, it definitely looked as if it used to be a factory. Jack just walked through the front door yelling for the clowns. Two slender, well-dressed men approached us. One of them angrily shouted, 'For the last time, fat man, we are Jokers.' The other shouted, 'Why have you brought this old man to our fortress?' I quickly intervened. 'Excuse me, gentlemen, but I think we can benefit from each other.' 'How exactly would that work, aged one?' one of them asked. I answered, 'Because even though this is a lovely factory, two outstanding gentlemen like yourselves should be leading a kingdom, not a factory. I can make this happen, but only if you help me find my wife.' The two Jokers thought for a moment, then one asked, 'And how do you plan on doing that?' I said, 'We simply trick the evil king into thinking you two are the real kings.' The other Joker said, 'Oh, we trick the king. That shouldn't be that hard. Why didn't we think of that?' Knowing they were being sarcastic, I continued. 'I will give you an army. Bigger than the kingdom warriors could stop. We'll confuse the king, and you'll reign in his spot.' The Jokers weren't very optimistic but agreed only if they could bring their sister and a witch. 'The more the merrier,' I agreed. 'And now there are six of us.'

"Meeting the sister and the witch for the first time was a little awkward. Fat Jack and the sister seemed to hit it off right away, while

I was still talking to the witch. All the witch wanted to talk about was Paradise. Having no idea what she was babbling about, I asked the Jokers. They explained that the Horizon was broken into three main parts, with some smaller parts sprinkled about. The kingdom was the bad part; the Here was where they worked, but the Paradise was just that—Paradise. All the good people were allowed in there. I quickly thought that's where Maggie must be. I must go find out. So, I had them stay at the factory, and soon I'd send them their army. They agreed to wait at the factory for my return."

Chapter 24
Part Three

"Always look on the brighter side of things; especially if it gets to dark." –Jim

"After a couple of days' walk and a lot of complaining from Jack, we reached the gates of Paradise. Jack knocked on the gates as I looked over the glorious walls that surrounded Paradise. It wasn't a long wait before a very small man yelled at us from the top of the wall.

"Do not touch the gate again! You are not welcome here, so leave at once."

Confused, I explained. "We're only here because I'm looking for my wife. Her name is Maggie. Do you know of her?"

The small man replied, "I know of no Maggie. You must leave now."

"Then I shall see the king."

The rude little man shouted, "There's no king of Paradise! There's only a queen, and she'll not talk with the likes of you."

I thought, *This is Paradise?* With nothing left to do, Jack and I climbed the hillside overlooking the Paradise walls and built a campfire. That night, I laid there, looking up at the stars. A weird twinkle caught my eye. It looked like a star was falling right toward us. I asked Jack if he could see it, but he was fast asleep, and nothing was waking him up. The star landed beside me. Its bright light faded as a shadowy figure stepped out of the star casing. The Shadow said, 'Jim, I've been watching you from above. I think we can both help each other. I will deliver Maggie to you if you remove a baby for me.' I'm confused as I question the shadowy figure. 'You want me to remove a baby? Like remove, remove.' The Shadow replied, 'Yes! I had a deal with Kannon, King of Evil, and Dayne, the Queen of Paradise. When they arrived here, they were lovebirds who fell on bad luck. I made a deal that they could stay in the Horizon forever if they vanquished the leader of stars. They agreed, and with my help, they ended the star leader's reign. Even though I cannot be a star leader, I can control the stars if there's no leader. Now that I have control, I gave them my word and let them remain in the Horizon. But, to keep them in line, I made Kannon King of the Dark Kingdom and Dayne Queen of Paradise. They were not allowed to be together. But true love made them break the deal, as they met at a small house in the Here. I was so mad I placed a spell on Kannon. He would never be allowed in Paradise, or he would lose Dayne forever. Little did I know, Dayne had delivered three babies. A boy who would follow in his father's footsteps and control the kingdom with him. A girl who would grow up in Paradise at her mother's side. And the last child was sent to the stars to become the star leader and replace me.' I asked how I could help in all this. He responded, 'You must eliminate star baby. This way, I'll control the sky forever. You, in return, will be rewarded with your precious Maggie.'

"I had no other choice but to accept the offer. As a celebration of our deal, the evil star offered me help in the form of soldiers. He forced all the stars to the Horizon and changed them to Shadow warriors. The stars were so terrified of the evil star, they did as they were ordered. The evil star also gave a safe place for me and Maggie to watch everything unfold. He sent me a park bench, which could only be seen by those I chose to see it. As he left, he said the baby would be sent to the Horizon soon, and I was to dispose of it immediately.

"I sat on the park bench with quite a dilemma. How was I going to eliminate a defenseless baby? Soon the stars began to crash to the ground, leaving me with hundreds and hundreds of Shadow soldiers. That actually woke up Jack. I asked the startled fat man to deliver the Shadow army to the Jokers at the factory. Jack agreed and he marched them off into the darkness."

Chapter 24
Part Four

"Never make a deal that you lose more than you gain." –Jim

Jim stops talking, as his mind seems to leave him for a bit. He watches as the cricket scuttles around the cell floor. Once the cricket stops, Jim collects his thoughts and continues.

"That next morning, just before the sun rose, I saw a final falling star. I knew that must be my objective. I ran to the area where it landed. As I approached it, there on the ground was a golden chest. It was locked, so I found a large rock and smashed the chest open. The lid rose, revealing a very sick-looking baby. I felt its head and could tell it was burning up with fever. I took the child in my arms, trying to ease its crying. Finally, I got it to stop crying and looked up to see seven knights standing around me. They were all dressed the same. Each one had a purple 'P' on the chest plate of their armor. One of the knights said, 'Sir, are you alright? Where did you get that child from?' Instantly I explained, 'This is my child sent from the stars.' Another knight said, 'Old man, this child is not yours. This child belongs to our queen. I order you to hand it over.' Sarcastically, I respond, 'Yeah, I'm pretty sure that's not going to happen. How about we try it this way? I'll stay here with the baby, and you go get your queen and bring her here.' Then I sat down on my bench and disappeared. The knights were dumbfounded. They thought I disappeared into thin air until they heard me speak once again. 'Now, go get your queen. Oh, and don't make us wait too long. This baby looks quite sick.'

"The knights ride off toward Paradise. Soon, they return with a beautiful young lady dressed in a purple and gold gown with teal ribbons. I knew this must be the queen. I offered her a spot on my bench, and she accepted, and we both vanished from the knights' sight. I handed her the baby as a sign of good faith. I then asked her about my Maggie, but she knew nothing about her. How did no one know of my beloved? The queen seemed to accept the sickness from the baby, as she looked deadly ill and the baby looked totally fine.

"I stepped from the bench, revealing myself to the knights. 'They've taken the queen and the baby!' The head knight anxiously looked around. 'Who? Who are you referring to?' I informed him, 'The Shadow army! They took them both. They went that way.' I pointed in the opposite direction than I sent Jack. The knights rode off in a cloud of dust, leaving me, the queen, and the baby alone."

The cricket doesn't seem like it wants to hear much more of the story, as it runs out of sight under the cell door. Jim must finish his story, even if his friend doesn't want to listen.

"So, I carried the queen and baby back to the Paradise gate. This time the small, rude guard let me in. While they were all tending to the ill queen, I noticed thousands of doors all in a line. I asked a passerby, 'What's with the doors?' He explained that each one of those doors led to our present world, and a couple were just transporters. Since everyone's attention was on the ill queen, I gathered twelve or so doors and shoved them through a transporter door, which I adjusted to send them to Jack's and my cave. Once I thought I'd sent enough doors, I grabbed the baby and stepped through. Sure enough, I was in the kitchen of my cave. Quietly, I placed the baby on my bed and then entered the transporter back to Paradise.

"I approached the sick queen and acted as if I knew what was wrong with her. I demanded everyone step back and give her room. 'Do not touch her or you'll catch it!' I yelled. Once I had a clear path to an open transporter, I picked the queen up and made a run for it. Jumping through the portal, we landed in the living room of a small empty house. I laid the ill queen on the couch and got her a glass of water. It's weird, but I thought the queen knew where she was. I smashed the teleport door so we couldn't be followed.

"Leaving the queen and the house, I headed for my cave to check on the baby. When I arrived, I found three beggars lurking around. In exchange for some food and a promise to make all three kings, they would take the baby into the woods and fulfill my deal with the evil star. The beggars took the child and vanished into the woods. Curiously, I stepped into the doors and retrieved some sorry souls, just in case I needed to change plans.

"So, you see, my friend, I control everything in the Horizon. Or, at least, I did."

Chapter 25

"Two steps forward, and three steps back. Four if you're little like Bug." –Spin Doll

Hunter holds Bee, refusing to release him to Dak.

Dak tells the Jokers, "We'll give him five seconds to hand over Bee before we start releasing his friends."

Then, facing Hunter, he says, "Hunter, I know how quick you are with that pool stick. But, with a sword placed to Spin Doll's head, I beg to differ that you're quick enough. Now, baby. Please. Five... four... three... two..."

Hunter hands Bee to Dak. Dak, not being stupid, makes Sin take the baby.

Bug blurts out, "What are you going to do with him?"

Sin, holding Bee up, sarcastically boasts, "Whatever we want to do, boy."

Bee reaches out and touches Sin's face, making Sin's mind watch part of his story. He sees himself looking at himself in a mirror. His reflection speaks to him, then steps out of the mirror. Sin is standing beside himself. He wonders what that means as he pulls away from Bee and rejoins the group. Feeling weird, he hands Bee to Omin.

Bee reaches up and touches Omin's face. His mind sees almost the same story Sin did. Only he is in the mirror and steps out of it beside Sin. Omin hands Bee to Cozzex and walks away confused.

Dak walks backward, not taking his eyes off Hunter. "Now, nothing will happen to the kid as long as you don't follow us."

Dak and the Jokers mount their unicorns. Cozzex can't hold Bee and mount her unicorn, so Dak makes Omin and Sin dismount and help her. Once they're all in the saddle, they ride off too quickly for Hunter to take a shot.

Jax, confused as to why they would need Bee, questions, "Why would they take him? They're heading back to where we came from."

Bug slams his bat on the ground. "I knew I didn't like that kid from the beginning. There was no way he could elude the Shadows for that long. How can Kannon and Dayne's kid be so evil? I'm telling you, Hunter, this place is supposed to bring everyone closer. But it's more like everyone's for themselves."

Spin Doll interrupts Bug. "We need to go save Bee."

Hunter holds his hands up and calmly adds, "We can't go back with us four. We'd be released before we reached Bee."

Spin Doll cries, "They will release him!"

Hunter shakes his head. "We need help. We can't help Bee if we're released. We go north and find help."

Spin Doll still insists, "No. I was chosen to save him. I'm going whether you go with me or not." She storms out and heads in the direction Dak went.

Hunter turns to Bug. "You go with her. Don't let her do anything stupid. I'll take Jax with me. We'll find help and meet up with you two at the kingdom gate."

Bug agrees as he runs off to catch up with Spin Doll. Hunter and Jax head north.

Reaching Spin Doll, Bug attempts to calm her down. "Spin Doll, slow down. You know Hunter is right. But you are right also. We need to rescue Bee, but we can't run in like crazed lunatics. We're extremely outnumbered, and they know we'll try and rescue Bee. They'll be waiting for us. I mean, I know I'm an animal when I get fired up, but..."

Spin Doll bursts out laughing and jokes, "What kind of animal are you?"

"I'm a tiger. No, I'm a bear."

Spin Doll again laughs and stops walking. "A bear? The only way you'd be bare is if you were naked. I'm picturing you as a mean prairie dog or a badger having a bad day."

Bug begins laughing with her. Being overtired, they laugh foolishly for ten minutes or so. Once they stop and begin walking again, Bug softly speaks, "I saw a show once. Prairie dogs can be mean."

Spin Doll begins giggling as she informs Bug, "Well, prairie dogs are cute as well."

Bug grabs her hand, and they continue walking.

Hunter and Jax are making good time as they jog at a steady pace. They come to the edge of the valley that was once home to the Never Lights. Hunter points out that it looks as if something was over there. But it must've been moved recently. They take off jogging once again.

Jax suddenly trips and falls into a hole. Hunter helps her up as she says, "Wow, that came out of nowhere. What made this big hole?"

Standing back from it, Hunter realizes what it is. "That's not a hole. It's a footprint."

"What thing has a foot that big?"

Hunter soon realizes there are many of those footprints. He swallows hard. "I don't know what made these, but let's hope they're on our side."

They continue jogging while weaving in and out of the giant footprints.

Chapter 26

"The greatest gift in life is giving someone life." –Char

Char and Dayne land near where she released the knights. Dayne slides off Char and begins yelling, "Megan, Megan, Megan—where are you?"

A rumble comes from a large group of thornbushes. Megan is stuck in the middle with no way out. She tries using the swords she retrieved from the bushes. The thorns are too close for her to get a good swing at them. Char takes a big breath and lights fire all around Megan, burning most but not all of the thorns. She clears enough for Dayne to reach Megan and help her out.

Megan, ecstatic about being out of those bushes, hugs Dayne, then turns to hug Char but freezes, not knowing if it's safe to hug a dragon.

Char yells, "Get over here, you!" She grabs Megan and hugs her.

Megan asks, "My queen, is this your dragon?"

"No one owns a dragon. This is my friend, Char."

Megan bows toward Char and politely introduces herself. "My name is Megan. Pleased to meet you, Char."

"It's nice to meet you as well, Megan."

Dayne looks at Char. "May I beg you for one more thing? Can you maybe fly us both to Paradise?"

Char places her tail on the ground and then lets them climb up on it. She takes to the air, and they're off.

Willow and the knights arrive at Megan's hiding spot just in time to see Char fly away. Stopping to take a quick rest, the knights find their swords in the chard bramble and are armed once more. After a quick drink, they're ready to head out again. Before they can leave, they hear someone running toward them. Each knight hides behind a tree or rock, waiting to pounce on the unsuspecting intruders. Hunter and Jax come running into the trap. The knights jump out, surrounding the joggers with their swords.

Hunter immediately informs them, "We're the good guys. Please don't hurt us."

Willow yells, "State your name and why you came running up on us!"

Jax responds, "I'm Jax, and this is Hunter. We're looking for some help to rescue a baby."

Russell inquires, "What's this about a baby?"

"A very bad man and a couple of Jokers took our baby."

Chet blurts, "They took your baby?"

Hunter shakes his head. "It's not our actual baby. The baby she's talking about is called the storyteller."

Willow interrupts. "Did you say storyteller? We must get this info to the queen at once."

Confused, Hunter asks, "Queen? There's no queen in the Horizon. There are four kings, and one is a lady. But I guarantee the kingdom doesn't have a queen."

Russell winces as he barks back at Hunter, "The kingdom! As in the refuge where the Dark King lives? Our queen would not reside in the refuge. Our home is called Paradise."

Hunter and Jax are now more confused than ever.

Willow orders the knights to march on to Paradise. Hunter and Jax follow, keeping their distance. As they walk, Hunter and Jax take in all the beauty of this unknown part of the Horizon that they knew nothing of.

Jax asks, "Did you know any of this existed?"

Hunter shakes his head as he continues taking it all in. Just before they crest this long hillside, the knights stop walking.

Willow walks back to the following pair. He begins to order them, just as he had his knights, "When we break over this ridge, you will notice the wall of Paradise. Do not touch the wall of Paradise. We will march along the wall till we reach the gates of pearls. We will then wait for the queen's permission to enter. Now, we will have a two-hour walk to the gate. The dark will fall upon us, so I recommend you march with us."

Hunter says, "You want us to walk with you? We accept."

Willow gives a slight smile, then returns to his knights along with two new members.

Reaching the crest, Hunter and Jax stand in awe. Giant gold walls seem to go on forever. Hunter and Jax must look goofy with their big grins because all the knights giggle at them. Russell pats Hunter on the back.

"Come on, bud, we've still got a ways to go."

They once again begin walking.

Meanwhile, Char, Dayne, and Megan land in front of the pearl gate. Dayne looks at Megan, giving her the go-ahead. "Megan, you know this place. Lead the way."

Megan responds, "My queen, this is your Paradise. You honestly don't recognize any of this?"

Dayne shakes her head and retorts, "This is all new to me."

The two girls climb off Char and thank her for the ride. Megan grapples with how to explain to Char that she can't fit through the gate. Dayne, realizing it, comments, "Char, that gate looks too small for you to enter. While we figure out what to do, I need one more favor that only you will know how to handle."

Char wonders what task Dayne could possibly have that only she could perform. So, she agrees, curious as to what it could be. Dayne pulls the small chest from her pouch. She slowly opens it as Megan and Char closely watch. The two think Dayne is losing it because there's nothing in the box. Dayne reaches into the chest and pulls out a beautiful gold and purple dragon's egg.

Char's eyes widen with the excitement of seeing the object. All the dragons have been gone for hundreds of years. She's been the only dragon in the Horizon for a long time. Dayne reaches out and hands the egg to Char. Char takes the egg from Dayne as a giant tear lands beside Megan, getting her wet. Char is actually crying, as she can't hold back her happiness.

Dayne orders Char, "Take this egg to a safe place. Please watch over it and guard it with your light. If and when it hatches, teach my dragon the ways of the ancient dragons. I'm sorry. I mean teach your baby the ways of the ancient ones."

Char can't believe the words coming from Dayne. Is it true— Dayne gave her a baby dragon?

Dayne hugs Char. "This is my gift to you. Thank you for everything you've done for us. I will never forget you, my friend."

Char takes to the air. She gives a wave and blows a heart in smoke toward the girls. Dayne and Megan wave back, then Char is gone into the sunset.

Out of sight, Megan asks Dayne, "You ready, my queen? Your Paradise awaits you."

Dayne nods, then they approach the gates of pearls.

Chapter 27

"The third times not the charm." –Cam

Reaching the kingdom gate, Dak and the Jokers dismount the unicorns then help Cozzex and Baby Bee off theirs. Sin slaps the unicorns on the ass, sending them into the woods.

A disgusted Dak barks out, "Why'd you do that? We could've used those unicorns."

"What do we need them for? It isn't like we can taken them in with us."

Omin rolls his eyes. "We could've taken them in with us. Why would you think they can't go in?"

Sin, trying to sound smart, replies, "Ahh, they can't dance. How would they get in?"

Cozzex lays Baby Bee on the ground to take a break from holding him. She shakes her arms, trying to get the feeling back in them.

Dak calls the three in to huddle with him. They need a plan before entering the kingdom and facing the kings. "Cozzex, I need you to change into Dayne. Then you and I will walk into the kingdom with the Jokers in front of us. We'll make it look as if we've captured the Jokers, and we'll walk right into the kingdom. Cozzex, as Dayne, you'll take your seat on your throne, then order me to take the Jokers to the dungeon. Next, instead of going to the dungeon, we'll head for the towers. Then we'll destroy each of the tower lights, diminishing the kings' power."

Cozzex changes into her version of Dayne as the three men clap in sync.

"Perfect!" Dak shouts.

None of them notice that Baby Bee has dozed off. Suddenly, Bee begins to float in midair, as if someone is holding him. The floating baby slowly begins to move away from the plotting crew. Dak catches the movement out of the side of his eye while the Jokers compliment Cozzex on her looks. Slowly, unseen to everyone, Dak pulls a dagger from his back pocket. In an instant, Dak fires the dagger between Sin and Omin. The dagger stops midair, just in front of Bee and floats beside him as Cam appears with the knife embedded in his back. Cam places Bee on the ground before collapsing to his knees. Trying to reach the dagger, which is well placed from his reach, Cam speaks to the four observers.

"Why does everything have to be bad? What happened to love and happiness? Why can't people offer a hand to hold? Is it really too much to ask?"

Dak approaches as he answers, "We no longer ask how we can help. Now it's a world of 'if you can't help us, we don't need you.' But before you leave us, Cam, I have a question. Are you a cat?"

Cam looks at Dak, puzzled.

Dak finishes, "Because you seem to have nine lives. Let's hope this will be the last. I'm tired of seeing your face."

The Jokers and Cozzex all begin to laugh. Dak holds up his hand for silence and continues. "Since you're finally going to leave us, let me explain a few things to you."

Dak grabs Cam by the face and makes him look him in the eyes. "None of your friends were released by accident. It was my blade that released them all. Dillo, sure, there were many cuts through his shell. None of you realized that every incision was the same size. Only two swords could penetrate that shell, Dayne's releaser and my eliminator."

Cam questions, "You were fighting up on the hill. How could you reach him?"

Dak laughs as he looks at Cozzex who simply changes form to look exactly like Dak.

"Cozzex was up on the hill, and the rest of you were so intrigued by Hoss' and the Beast's battle. Really, I couldn't believe how many times I had to bury my blade into his back. Who would've thought I'd miss Bug with them all? I have to give it to Dillo; he was a tough simpleton."

Cam, beginning to lose his light, turns toward Bee and repeats himself, "I'm so sorry, Bee. I'm so sorry."

Dak laughs. "Wait, Cam, I'm not finished. It's funny, but you and Hoss will be released in the same manner. My blade in your back. I had Spin Doll dragged off so I could make her scream with that beautiful voice."

Dak squeezes Cam's face harder and continues, "Oh, and trust me, she'll scream. Lakin seemed to be the only one I didn't have the pleasure of releasing. But no matter. She wasn't important anyway. Putting that snake scent on Colt without her noticing—that was a plan that worked better than even I could imagine. The pain she endured for so long couldn't be any more enjoyable. I had all I could do to keep from smiling. Then she released herself for your weak ass, which gave me a two-for-one."

Cam tries to crawl toward Bee, but Dak stops him by placing his boot on Cam's face. "Show me some tears, and I'll end you quicker."

Cam, trying to look at Bee, replies, "I think I've run out of tears between this world and my last one. So, not to sound rude, I'm pretty sure you're not going to see me cry. But if I may have one last request..."

Dak smiles at the Jokers. "Oh, this is going to be rich. Okay, Camy, old boy. What's your last request?"

Cam, with what little breath he has left, states, "My last request is that you and your two pals kiss my ass."

The three bullies notice a grin form on Cam's face. Furious over Cam's request, Dak stomps his boot, crushing Cam's face in. They all laugh as they watch Cam's light rise in the air.

Having Cozzex turn into Cam's lookalike, Dak orders her to take Bee to Bug, Spin Doll, and Hunter. When they least expect it, she is to release all three, then Bee. Cozzex scoops Bee in her arms and heads out to complete Dak's plan. Dak gathers the Jokers and heads into the kingdom.

Chapter 28

"True words were lost on a cricket." –Jim

Jim loses his place because the cricket continues running in and out of the cell, making him forget what he's saying. Once the cricket finally stops moving and seems to find a good place to relax, Jim remembers his discussion and begins again. "So, you see, friend, we couldn't just run around here with a queen and a baby. It would bring too much attention. We came across an old farmer and his wife. They were kind enough to let us stay in their barn for the night and out of sight. Jack snuck into the old lady's closet and took an outfit that looked as if it hadn't been worn for quite some time. Before Dayne could revive herself, we changed her into the outfit and buried her queen's attire under the hay in the barn. When Dayne awoke, we fabricated this big story about her and Kannon. Since she had caught the same sickness as the baby, she would believe anything. I had Jack keep the baby hidden from Dayne so the two never saw each other."

With the cricket still sitting there, listening intently, Jim continues. "The next morning, Queen Dayne awoke to find just me sitting with her. She seemed to feel a little better, so I talked her into walking back to the cave. The entire time we walked, I couldn't help worrying about what Jack was going to do with the baby. Returning to the cave, we were greeted by Jack, sitting outside the cave alone. I explained that this cave was part of our home and that she could stay as long as she liked. When she went into the cave to inspect it, I pulled Jack to the side and asked him what he did with the baby. Jack said, 'Relax. I stuck the baby in one of the doors.' Not knowing what he meant, Jack showed me a line of doors that were now in our cave. Confused, I asked him why they were there. He said, 'I met this witch, who was not the nicest lady. She offered me a job. She said if I would keep these doors hidden, she would grant me one wish. So, not wanting to lose a wish, I agreed to hide the doors in our cave.' Not letting him know it was I who sent the doors, I then questioned him about the baby. He said, 'I put the baby in one of the doors. The only thing is, I don't remember which door.' I then asked him if the witch had granted his wish. 'I think so,' he replied. Upset about him losing the baby, I barked back at him, 'What do you mean you think so? Either she did or she didn't.' Jack simply responded, 'I asked for a way to remove all the people who annoyed me. She informed me that when I woke up in the morning, my wish would be granted. Also, she left me two sets of keys for the doors.'

"The very next morning, we woke up to Jack, having a mouth full of metal teeth. Not understanding at that moment how Jack having metal teeth was a way to get rid of the people who bothered him, we soon learned a young man annoyed Jack. I watch Jack's head deform as he picked the man up and ate him. Let me tell you, it was quite disgusting the first few times.

"After a few days passed, and the witch returned, I questioned her about Jack's eating habits. Her only response was, 'He got what he asked for.' Not happy that she turned my friend into this nightmarish creature, I demanded she give me three wishes since the cave was actually mine, or I would have eaten by her own devise. Sighing with annoyance, she agreed and asked me what I requested. My first wish was to have her show me where Maggie was. All that time I searched for her, and she wasn't even in the Horizon. She lived and was still back in our world. That enraged me so much that I wanted to destroy the Horizon. So, my first wish became Dak. I wanted both the King of Despair and the Queen of Promise to both have what they couldn't have. A love so strong that they could never have. That way they could feel the same pain I was feeling. She bowed her head and stated that it had been done. Kannon, the King of Despair and Darkness, will be condemned in the Refuge forever. The queen, Dayne, will reside forever in Paradise. They will never be able to have one another but can love no one except each other. Not known to me, the witch made a son from stolen hair from both Kannon and Dayne. This son was named

Dak. Dak stands for Destruction and Kindness. With good and evil in Dak's body, his inner war with both sides will drive him nuts.

"My next wish was to give power to those who didn't deserve it. The witch then took three bumbling idiots and made them believe they were kings. That is where the kings came into the picture. Everyone soon thought they were the true kings of the Horizon. But, trust me, their reign couldn't last long.

"The third and final wish was to remove all the stars from the sky. If Maggie and I couldn't sit under them, then no one would. The witch granted my wish, making all the stars crash to the ground. The smashed and broken stars released the souls they held. These souls were angry that they'd been disturbed from their final resting spots. Their anger changed them to dark, hate-filled Shadows. These Shadows wanted to remove any happiness they saw. Soon, they all gathered in the Refuge, following King Kannon. So, with my deal with the image of the star-like leader dropping the stars, and the witch destroying them when they reached the ground, worked perfectly. It's best to cover all your angles. Making Dak out of one of the three children given to Dayne and Kannon would tear them apart.

"With all the wishes granted, the witch quickly said goodbye. But before leaving, she said, 'All this can be changed by eight unknowns, plus Kanon and Dayne to make ten heroes. If we go through the doors and retrieve them, they may restore the Horizon.' Not realizing the chaos we caused, we soon found the Horizon to be a dangerous place. We entered the doors and tried to retrieve the heroes, but they weren't willing to come to help. So, we tormented eight people who were easily having issues of their own. We dragged them here and made them think they were some kind of great warriors. They believed it so much, they willed themselves special powers."

Jim stops talking and glances at the cricket, who is staring intently. "Oh, you want to know how Kannon becomes one of them. Every day, he and Dayne stood in their highest towers. They stood there for hours just looking at each other, both wanting to hold the other in their arms. One day, Kannon stood looking, but Dayne as nowhere to be found.

Rumors reached his ears that Dayne was kidnapped and was with a child. Kannon left the refuge kingdom in search of his only love, standing outside his kingdom wall in the Here. His punishment for leaving the kingdom was he would be stripped of his identity and powers. He no longer knew any of it, thanks to the three kings and the witch, who made their own deal. The only thing he could remember was his love for Dayne. He soon met up with us, and my quick thinking led to me telling him a story of another life he had had with Dayne back in my world. To my surprise, they all believed my stories wholeheartedly.

"So, this is my story. I have nothing left. No power, no fake brother, no friends, and most of all, no Maggie. Look at me—locked up talking to a friggin' cricket."

Jim looks around his cell, not wanting to talk to the cricket anymore. It is eerily quiet. Suddenly, a familiar voice speaks from the cell window.

"Well, isn't this just pathetic?"

Another voice adds, "Is that the mighty Jim, sitting with all his friends?"

Chapter 29

"A small reunion makes for a great surprise." –Hunter

Standing in front of the gates, Dayne has no clue how they're going to enter. She sees no doorbell or knocker. "How do we open the pearl gates?"

Megan smiles. "Just walk up and touch the gates. Then watch what happens."

Dayne cautiously approaches the giant gates. Slowly, she reaches up and places her hand on the front of it then quickly pulls her hand away and backs up. The gates begin to rumble, then everything stops, and all is quiet again.

Dayne asks Megan, "Why didn't it open? It sounded as if it were opening."

Megan just giggles as she points to the top of the wall. Dayne glances up and sees a small man's hand pop up.

"Who dares touch my walls?"

Dayne nervously responds, "Excuse me, sir. My name is Dayne, and this is Megan."

The little man remarks, "Sorry, I don't have a Dayne on my list. Please step aside and be gone."

Megan yells, "Owl, are you really not smart enough to see this is the queen?"

Owl bends down toward the girls, squinting his eyes. "Who dares talk to the great Owl like that?"

"Owl, you better put your glasses on and recognize the queen. She is quickly losing her patience."

The girls watch as the little man places his glasses on his face. Owl's eyes just about pop out of his head when he clearly sees Dayne. Stuttering, he says, "My queen! I... I am truly sorry. Let me get those gates open."

Owl disappears, and the girls can hear him yelling on the other side of the gate. "Quickly, you there. Help me open the gates. Hey everyone, the queen has returned."

A crowd's cheers erupt and, once again, a rumbling sound comes from the gate. Light shoots out from the forming crack as the gates widen. Dayne is surprised as the almost-too-bright-to-see light hits her eyes. Both girls try to block the light with their hands. But the gates stop and begin to close again.

Owl appears back at the top of the walls once again without his glasses. "My ladies, I'm once again sorry. But someone is approaching. You must defend yourselves."

Dayne, without thinking, raises the releaser as Megan draws her sword as well. They brace themselves for the oncoming crowd. Closer and closer the group storms toward them.

Dayne orders Megan, "Megan, stay behind me."

Megan replies, "Don't worry about me, my queen. I'm also quite skilled with a blade."

With the charging group closing in, Dayne believes she recognizes one of them.

"Dayne! Is that really you?"

From the voice, she instantly knows it's Hunter.

Megan smiles as she informs Dayne, "It's our soldiers and two others."

Hunter runs up to her and pulls her into a hug. "Dayne! You're safe."

The two embrace for a few seconds as Willow checks on Megan. Hunter releases Dayne and introduces Jax. "Dayne, this here is Jax. Jax was one of Spin Doll's friends back in their world. She helped get Baby Bee back to the Horizon."

Dayne hugs Jax. "Pleased to meet you, Jax. Thank you for everything you've done. Any friend of Spin Doll is a friend of ours."

"Thank you, my queen."

Hunter chuckles. "Dayne isn't a queen. She's the first lady king."

Willow interjects. "Mr. Hunter, this is the Queen of Paradise. And you will address her as such."

Hunter looks at Dayne with one eyebrow raised.

Dayne leans over and whispers,, "For some reason, they think I'm the queen of whatever is on the other side of this wall."

Russell adds, "My queen, we must not dally. The quicker we're behind that wall, the better."

Chapter 30

"It isn't the shine that makes a ring beautiful; it's the reason for the ring." –Bug

Spin Doll and Bug, exhausted and hungry, continue walking toward the kingdom. Bug can tell from the look on her face how upset she is from losing Baby Bee. It hurts him to see her like this.

"Let's stop for a bit and rest. Maybe I can find us some food. You can start a fire and find us a soft place to rest."

Spin Doll doesn't want to stop, but she knows they need a rest and some food. She thinks, *Even if we continue, we'll be too weak to do anything when we get there!* So, she agrees and begins to pick up some wood for the fire. Bug runs off into the woods in search of food.

Spin Doll finds a nice spot and quickly builds a fire and soon has it burning well. The heat is a little intense, so she backs away and makes a nice spot for them to sit. Bug returns with an armful of items. He names each one as he places them in front of Spin Doll.

"I found some mushrooms, a couple of wild carrots, snails, crickets, and some kind of red berry. I'm pretty sure we can eat them."

Spin Doll laughs as she grabs for the carrots and a big mushroom.

"What, no snails or crickets?"

Spin Doll shakes her head. "I'll pass on the bugs. I've become a vegetarian."

Bug jokes, "I hope I'm not one of the bugs you don't want."

Spin Doll giggles. "We'll see. It all depends on how well you cook this food."

Bug finds a flat rock and places it in the center of the fire. Next, he sets the mushrooms and snails on the rock to cook. Jokingly, he says, "Rare or well done? I can't promise anything. I'm not that good of a cook. In our old world, I couldn't make toast without burning it. But if you're looking for someone to make a fluffernutter, I'm your guy."

"A fluffernutter? Never heard of it. Are you messing with me?"

With surprise, Bug yells, "You've never had a fluffernutter? First, you take two nice, soft slices of bread. Then you cover one of the slices with a thick layer of peanut butter. Then take the other slice and cover it with fluff. Fluff is kind of like melted marshmallows. Finally, you take both slices and firmly press them against each other. Then, TADA, you have yourself a fluffernutter."

Spin Doll laughs as Bug acts like he's eating a huge sandwich. After eating everything but the red berries, because neither of them knows if they're safe or not, they sit snuggling in the glow of the fire. Quietly they sit and watch the flames dance as night returns. Bug sits against an old log while Spin Doll sits between his legs with her back against his chest, Bug's arms wrapped around her. Neither of them wants to be anywhere else but there.

The flames lower a bit as Spin Doll speaks. "Our last world and the Horizon will take our souls. But my heart, my heart, will always be yours. Even when I'm gone, I will still be with you."

Bug replies, "Not that you will ever leave, but if that day does come, just know I will be the only man in the Horizon missing a piece of his heart. Promise me, if we go, we will go together. Because without you, I don't want to be here."

Bug hugs her a little tighter. The two sit again quietly watching the fire dance.

Spin Doll can feel that something is on Bug's mind. She leans her head back to see his eyes. This gives Bug the courage to ask, "Spin Doll, do you think if we had met back in our world, we would be just like we are now?" He looks at the empty sky. "Why, if we were meant for each other, did our world not have us meet? If I had met you, I would've never jumped—I mean fallen off that bridge."

Spin Doll kisses his cheek. "If we had met and you had jumped, I would've caught you."

Bug smiles. "Back in our world, if I had asked you to go to the prom with me, do you think you would have?"

"Yes, definitely! I would have worn a beautiful, long dress. You would have been in a handsome-looking suit. When we walked into that room, all eyes would've been on us."

Bug grins as he tightens his hug. "After the prom—a few years down the road—do you think if I had asked you to marry me, you might have said yes?"

Spin Doll nods, confirming that she would have.

Bug releases one arm as he reaches in his pocket. Fumbling for a moment, he eventually pulls something out. With a large gulp, he holds up a makeshift ring in the fire's light. Spin Doll's eyes widen as she reaches her hand up to it. Smiling, she states, "Bug, it's beautiful."

Bug shyly answers, "Aw, it's not much. Just a couple of Starletta bottle tops that I formed into a ring. Back in our world, it would have had a diamond in it."

"I think it's one of the most beautiful rings I have ever seen."

Bug works his way out from behind Spin Doll and takes a knee in front of her. He holds the ring toward her as he nervously says, "You are the most beautiful girl I've ever seen. I never knew that I was missing a part of my heart until I saw those eyes looking at me. That day, at the top of the barn, my body was full of fear. It was until you looked at me. The fear left my body, and I knew if I saved you, I would save myself. Spin Doll, I have nothing in this world or in the last, but if you would have me for your husband, I would now have everything. Spin Doll, will you be my wife?"

Spin Doll, with tears rolling down her cheeks, responds, "Oh, Bug, my handsome Bug. I would want nothing more than to be your wife. Yes! Yes! A million times, yes!"

Bug struggles, through his blurry eyesight, to place the ring on Spin Doll's finger. It is a perfect fit. Once the ring is firmly on her finger, they slowly lean in to kiss and make it official.

Just as their lips touch, they're interrupted by Cam's voice.

"Wow, that was awesome. Congratulations to both of you."

Bug and Spin Doll turn to see their friend standing there, holding Baby Bee.

Chapter 31

"Karma has a way of making you smile." –Jim

From his cell, a surprised Jim, yells, "You two idiots are still alive?"

Sin replies, "For now, but we seem to be doing better than you."

Jim barks back, "Get me out of here!"

Omin calmly answers, "Well, it looks like the tables have turned. It seems we're needed to save your pathetic life."

Jim growls as he tries to shake the cell door. Both Jokers step back, scared. Sin quickly reaches up and unlocks door. It swings open, revealing a mad, red-faced Jim. He steps out of the cell, slamming the door shut behind him, then locks it so no one notices that it's empty.

The cricket crawls out from under the door and stops beside Jim, who acts as if he doesn't see it.

He turns to the Jokers. "Who are you two here with? The fake kings are getting way too full of themselves. They're letting their newfound power go to their heads."

Sin replies, "We came here with Dak. Did you know how evil he is? He's actually frightening us."

Jim smiles as he mumbles, "Looks like the apple doesn't fall far from the tree. Where are the rest of them?"

Omin fills Jim in on the rest. "Dak has released almost all of them. Lakin, Colt, Cam, Dillo, Hoss..."

"What about Kannon and Dayne?"

Sin explains, "Kannon was released. As far as Dayne is concerned, no one has seen her. But we did see Hunter, Bug, and Spin Doll. Dak sent our sister to release them. She's probably already completed that task."

Jim is confused. "Your sister is still with us? I thought you two released her."

Omin chuckles. "You really thought we'd release our sister? What'd you think, we're monsters? Right this minute, she's pretending to be Cam."

"Our concern is not any of them. We need to stop that baby from reaching Paradise and freeing the stars and Kannon," Jim worriedly mutters.

Sin asks, "Our sister has the babe? But once she eliminates the group, she'll release the baby."

Jim grabs Sin's chest and pulls him close. "If that baby reaches Paradise, we're all done. If Kannon is freed, we're toast. There is no evil stronger than him. He will surely end us all."

Omin pushes Jim away from his brother. "Listen, old man, Dak is just as powerful. We need to leave this place, and soon."

"The only one who can stand up to those two is Hangman," Jim says. "Have you heard anything about his whereabouts?"

Sin, joking, responds, "A merchant in the square foolishly was saying something about a dragon tearing him apart and dispersing his body in different locations."

Jim shakes Sin by the shoulders. "You two must find his parts and restore him. It is our only chance against either Kannon or Dak. Go! Time is a premium." Jim points to an exit door, gesturing for the Jokers to leave immediately. As the Jokers exit, Jim says to himself, "Now to even the score with the kings."

Jim turns toward the cricket. Without a thought, he picks it up and puts it in his pocket, then exits the dungeon. While walking away, Jim hears a loud crash. Knowing the spiders must've broken the wall to his cell and will soon free themselves from the dungeon, Jim quickens his steps and is soon out of sight.

* * *

Dak knocks on Truncheon's door.

"You may enter."

Dak enters, slowly closing the door behind him.

Truncheon loudly voices, "You! How dare you enter my quarters.

127

We banished you from our kingdom. Leave now before I have you quartered in the kingdom square."

Dak chuckles devilishly. "Oh, I'll leave, but you most definitely will not."

Drawing his sword, Dak charges toward Truncheon and impales the king through his stomach. Blue goo gushes out, and Truncheon's eyes widen as he tries to speak but can't. Dak puts his finger to Truncheon's mouth, gesturing for him to remain silent. The king slowly vanishes and his light floats up to the sky. Dak picks up the king's crown and holds it up as if it were a trophy he has just won. After a few minutes, he tosses the crown to the ground while muttering, "Paper king."

The crown brightly shines as it begins to shake. Before Dak can react, the crown flies up and wraps itself around Dak's right wrist, forming into a bracelet. Dak feels an evil power flow through his veins. He leaves Truncheon's room and heads toward Furrow's room.

Reaching Furrow's room, Dak can hear more than one voice inside. Debating whether to enter or not, Dak and the bracelet can't wait any longer and barge through the door. A surprised Furrow and Paragon quickly grab their swords.

Furrow yells, "Have you gone mad, son?"

Dak, smiling, circles closer as he responds, "I'm not your son, but I am the one who's going to free you."

Paragon circles to the left side of Dak as Furrow circles to the right. Dak can see the fear in the once penniless, now kings' faces.

Furrow, in a low, slow voice, begs, "Dak, this doesn't have to end this way. We can still make you the fourth king."

"I can't be the fourth when there are only two kings. You see, Truncheon had to leave us." Dak taps his sword on the bracelet.

Furrow charges Dak as their swords meet with a loud clank. Paragon runs out the door, leaving Furrow to fend for himself.

Dak adds, "Looks like your buddy doesn't want to be released today. But don't fret; you'll be leaving soon to join Truncheon."

Repeatedly, the two swords clash together, neither gaining the upper hand.

Furrow tries reasoning. "Dak, listen to me. If Kannon gets released from his bubble prison, he will come after us. Trust me, with him being so powerful, we'll all need to work together to beat him."

Dak lowers his sword. "I believe you might be right. For now, we must work together. But when we are rid of Kannon, we'll continue this."

Relieved, Furrow lowers his sword and extends his hand to shake on it. With a smile, Dak places his sword back in its place and extends his hand while grasping an unseen dagger from his backside. The two shake hands as Dak pulls Furrow in for a hug.

Furrow, with a big sigh, whispers, "Truce."

Before anything else can be said, Furrow feels a sharp pain pierce into the middle of his back as Dak's dagger drives into it. Unable to speak, Furrow's eyes look through Dak as his life leaves his body. Dak catches Furrow's crown before it hits the ground. The crown fuses itself with the other crown, making Dak even more powerful.

* * *

Jim can't believe his eyes. Is Paragon running toward him? Paragon's eyes meet Jim's. Seeing his one-time friend, Paragon begs Jim to save him from Dak, yelling almost too quickly for Jim to understand. "Save me, my friend! Dak has become too powerful and is seeking to rid us kings."

The sly-thinking Jim quickly yells, "Hurry, into the dungeon! There are too many cells for him to check all of them."

Before Paragon can answer, Jim quickly opens the door to the dungeon and pushes Paragon inside, slamming the door closed behind him. Paragon turns and thanks his friend for helping him. Jim locks the door from the outside. Paragon looks through the small window in the door, which is covered with glass and metal bars.

Paragon yells loud enough for Jim to hear him. "Thank you, my friend. I will never forget this."

Jim yells back, "No problem, my friend. Think of it as we're even."

A little puzzled, Paragon watches Jim walk away. Relieved that his friend has helped him, Paragon turns and sits on the ground with his back against the door. Sitting there quietly so Dak doesn't find him, Paragon hears a sound slowly coming toward him. With very little light in the dungeon, he draws his sword. Before he can react, thousands of baby Octoros charge him. Swinging blindly, a single scream can be heard before he is engulfed. Paragon's sword falls to the dungeon floor with a single clank. In a matter of seconds, the king is no more.

Hearing the single scream brings a large smile to Jim's face before he disappears into the Shadows.

Chapter 32

"Theres nothing like getting home after a long trip." –Dayne

Hunter, too impatient, yells at Owl, "We're waiting!"

Owl gives a slight glance toward Hunter and circles Dayne one last time, finally stopping in front of her. Dropping to one knee, Owl says, "My queen has arrived."

The group cheers with excitement as they begin to take a knee. With everyone but Hunter, Jax, and Dayne kneeling, Owl clears his throat, sternly looking at Hunter and Jax to join them in kneeling. Realizing this, Hunter and Jax join the group in kneeling.

Dayne, now blushing and a little embarrassed, addresses the group. "Please stand up and be equal. If I truly am the queen of Paradise, then I make a new creed. Never will any man, woman, or child be better than another. We are all equal in the light of Paradise. Love will be the only thing to pass through these gates."

The group rises to their feet and follows Dayne toward the open gates. With such a bright light, Dayne can only imagine what she's about to step into.

Once through, the light vanishes, revealing the most beautiful sights anyone could ever dream. Waterfalls trickle from above as birds sing majestic songs. Hunter's first thought is that if there were a final resting place, this is what it would look like. Everything is perfect...except one thing.

Dayne, puzzled, asks Owl, "Where are the people? No one is here."

Owl takes the queen's hand and begins to explain. "My queen, when the stars fell to the ground, the center star fell as well."

"What do you mean, the center star?"

"The center star is the brightest star in the sky. It holds every star. When the center star crashed in the Horizon, it transformed into a sick child. You tried everything to rid the child of its sickness. Nothing worked. Not knowing the fate of the child, you named it Bee."

Hunter interrupts. "Why Bee?"

Owl continues while glaring at Hunter. "The baby was named Bee for the simple fact that some people see it as a girl, and some see it as a boy."

Jax jumps in. "But why Bee?"

Owl scowls at her now as he answers. "Our queen's reason for the name Bee was for the simple fact that when you see a bee, you can't tell if that bee is a boy or girl. So, the name Bee was given."

Dayne questions, "Where is the baby now?"

Owl looks toward the gate. "Out there."

Russell joins the conversation. "So, if we find this sick Bee, how do we return it to the center star?"

For some reason, Dayne knows the answer. "When the Bee is no longer sick and inside the Paradise walls, rumors are that it will return to being the center star and will take with it all the released lights and previous stars and place them in the sky."

Hunter interrupts once more. "I saw the Baby Bee. Shit. I held her. She was taken by Dak."

Owl shouts, "Dak! Oh, this isn't good. Dak is pure evil. He's the son of Kannon, the King of Fear. The evilest man in the Horizon."

Hunter barks out, "Kannon is my friend."

Before he can say another word, the knights pull their swords and point them toward Hunter.

Dayne immediately orders, "You will return your swords! If any of you ever draw your sword on him again, it most definitely will be your last. Have I made myself clear?"

The knights return their swords as quickly as they drew them.

Russell begins to apologize. "My queen, we were only trying to protect you."

Dayne snaps back, "Protect me? If you were trying to protect me, you would've been out in the Here protecting me." She points at Hunter as she continues. "This man protected me. He and his friends. Yes, even

Kannon and Dak saved me. These so-called Kings of Fear risked their lives for me. Some made the ultimate sacrifice. Those who gave their lights to bring me to this point will be known forever. I want statues of each and every one of them placed in the center of Paradise. This will be known as the 'Live Life as a Legend' garden. These warriors once gave up on themselves, but they never gave up on me."

Owl writes down every word Dayne speaks.

The gates crash shut, startling the group. Owl tries to explain to Dayne that under no circumstance is she to leave Paradise again. Dayne agrees, even though she knows she can't keep that promise.

As they begin to tour Paradise, Owl stops Dayne, Hunter, and Jax in front of a line. Holding his hands out, he says, "My queen, once we step over this line, all of Paradise will reveal itself. Your loyal subjects, houses, parks, buildings, and more will return to Paradise."

Puzzled, Dayne questions, "Where'd they go?"

Owl laughs. "They've always been here; they've just been hidden to the eyes. One last-ditch effort to protect Paradise and everything in it."

Excited and nervous, the three step over the line together. Wow, the sights they see. Bustling, beautiful towns and parks. Paradise is filled with people and animals as far as they can see. With so much love and happiness to feel, they can't help but smile.

Suddenly, Dayne feels a feeling in her stomach that seems to spread through her body. Soon she's engulfed in a beautiful light. Hunter and Jax must cover their eyes from the blinding light. After a few seconds, the light retracts, leaving Dayne standing in a beautiful purple dress covered in diamonds that glisten with shimmers of every color. She has long black hair and a golden staff with wings on the end of it. Hunter and Jax are stunned by her beauty. Tears fill their eyes as they drop to their knees. The calmness and joy that fill their bodies is more than they can hold back.

Dayne speaks in a different tone, as if she's a whole other person. "Rise, my friends. Embrace Paradise. For you are now a part of it."

The two stand and hug Dayne, knowing that they're free from hate, sorrow, and depression—that they're home. Releasing the tight-gripped hug, Dayne suggests they go and explore Paradise while she tends to some things. The two scamper off to do just as she's asked.

Once they're out of sight, Dayne turns toward Owl and sternly orders, "The knights must find that baby! Send only three: Maverick, Russell, and Megan. Leave the rest and prepare to defend Paradise."

"Defend Paradise? But you're back. We are all safe."

Dayne looks down at Owl. "No one is safe until we have the Bee and Dak is released. Also, I've located our twenty missing doors. They are in a cave in the southern part of the Here. Send the door watchers to gather them and return them to their place. It is not safe to leave them unattended."

Owl asks, "Do you know who stole them?"

Dayne nods. "Yes, that old man and his brother. Their names are Jim and Fat Jack."

"Have they been dealt with accordingly?"

"Fat Jack is no longer with us, but Jim is still out there."

Owl runs off yelling, "I will deal with it immediately."

Dayne stands alone, gazing over all of Paradise.

Chapter 33

"It's not always good to find what you're looking for." –Sin

"I can't believe Dak has us traipsing all over. We've covered the Horizon from corner to corner," Sin complains.

Omin responds, "Not only that, but we must lug this worthless body around. I'll tell you what, if we don't find his head somewhere on this hot, smelly beach, then I give up."

Sin, shaking his head, replies, "I don't know why he even needs Hangman when he's got us. Shit, two crazies are better than one."

Omin points down the beach. "Let's ask these guys. Maybe they've seen the head."

The two Jokers drop the bag of body parts behind them and approach the two gentlemen sunbathing. One man is skinny, and the other is not.

Sin approaches and says, "Excuse me, guys, but any chance you've seen anything strange around here?"

The heavy guy laughs. "Besides you two incredibly pale individuals? Nah, can't say we have."

Omin, not thinking that's funny, barks, "We are looking for a head."

The large guy answers, "Aren't we all, my friend? Aren't we all." The two strangers bump fists and laugh at their reply.

Sin, now red-faced from anger, yells, "Hey, funny man, maybe I should stop you from smiling! When we ask you a question, you answer it."

The two men stop laughing and stand up in front of the Jokers. The skinny man is about five inches taller than the Jokers, and the heavy man isn't much smaller. When standing, the heavy man is huge, possibly weighing four hundred pounds.

The skinny man sternly says, "What's your name, mouth? You see, we like to know the names of the asses we're about to kick."

Sin and Omin begin to roll up their sleeves as Omin answers, "His name is Sin and I'm Omin. Trust me, pal, you'll remember our names after this."

As they move in closer, the heavy guy adds, "This tall drink of water is Spazz, and I'm Bob. That stands for Big Old Boy."

The four men begin swinging with neither side gaining the upper hand. While in the scuffle, not one of them notices a head roll by them toward the bay. With a couple of lucky shots, Spazz and Bob knock Sin and Omin to the ground. That's when they notice a body slowly coming together behind the fallen Jokers. Spazz and Bob begin stepping backward as the body forms and approaches the Jokers from behind. Sin and Omin are puzzled as to why the men are backing up—until two big hands engulf each of their heads.

With the Jokers on one knee trying to catch their breath, the hands wrapping around their heads startle them. The hands pick the Jokers up, leaving their feet dangling. The Jokers finally realize who the hands belong to. Finally, they've fully restored Hangman.

Relieved, Sin orders, "Put us down, you imbecile! Boy, you're as smart as you look."

Omin must open his mouth as well. "Since we're the ones who found you, I demand you release us."

The Hangman does not release the grip. Sin demands, "Put us down at once! You are now our property. Do as you're told, boy."

Still dangling in the air, Hangman increases his grip. Spazz and Bob are at the other end of the beach and almost out of sight.

Omin nervously tries to reason with Hangman. "Look, you put us down and we'll take you back to the kingdom. When we arrive, you can help us eliminate Dak. Then, with us in power, we'll let you have whatever your evil little heart will desire. Now do we have a deal?"

The Hangman begins squeezing harder, and blood begins to trickle down both Jokers' faces. The Jokers scream for help so loudly that even Spazz and Bob can hear—and they're out of sight. Soon, the screaming stops as the lifeless bodies hang from the blue goo-covered hands of Hangman. Both bodies slowly turn into orbs and float into the sky. The Hangman drops the remains on the ground, turns toward the kingdom, and begins walking.

Spazz and Bob stop running as Bob tries to catch his breath with any air he can suck in.

Spazz says, "The screaming stopped. We must go to Paradise and tell the queen of this new threat."

Bob nods, still trying to collect oxygen. The two walk off the beach and into the brush as the ocean waves run up the beach and wash away the blue goo and the remains of the Jokers.

Chapter 34

"A love lost, can be an ultimate sacrifice." –Spin Doll

Spin Doll quickly takes Bee from Cam as Cam shakes Bug's hand, congratulating the two. Imposter Cam adds, "I knew you were perfect for each other right from the beginning."

Bug hugs the imposter Cam. "Cam, you always seem to pop up at just the right time." The two laugh and join Spin Doll and Bee.

Spin Doll is curious how Cam retrieved Bee from Dak, the two Jokers, and Cozzex. Stumped by the thoughts, she asks him, "Cam, how did you get Baby Bee from that group of lowlifes?"

Not happy with being called a lowlife, Cozzex replies, "When the idiots stopped to rest, I used my invisible spell and snuck off with it."

Bug laughs. "With your spell? What, now you're a magician?"

Spin Doll seems to think Cam is acting a bit strange. Instead of waiting and resting, they all agreed it would be best to get Bee to Paradise as soon as possible. Picking up their belongings, they're on their way.

Spin Doll, still concerned about Cam's demeanor, thinks she'll ask a few more questions while they walk.

"So Cam, how many times have you been revived since you got here?"

Cozzex, trying to be slick, answers, "Two—just like everyone else, I reckon."

Bug laughs and boasts, "You reckon? When the hell did you ever talk like that? And did you say twice? Shit, I can count at least three that I know of."

Cozzex tries to correct herself. "Yeah, it's been a few. I was just trying not to rub it in."

Spin Doll is sure now that something is wrong. "It's a shame you died by hit and run in your first life."

Cozzex tries to play along. "Yeah, it was my own fault. My parents told me to wear bright colors while walking at night."

Bug stops and looks at Cam. "What, are you trying to mess with my head? You never got hit by a car. You passed away because of cancer."

Cozzex now realizes that Spin Doll is catching on to her lies. She knows that Spin Doll must be the first one to go, and quickly, before Bug catches on as well. She blurts out, "We've been walking a lot. Mind if we stop for a rest for a minute? My feet are killing me."

Bug agrees and they stop in a small clearing. Spin Doll sits Bee beside Bug and goes off to use the ladies' room. Once Spin Doll is out of sight, Cozzex walks over and picks Bee up.

Bug quickly says, "I don't know if I'd pick that baby up without asking Spin Doll first. She's pretty protective of that little guy."

Cozzex places the baby back into its place, but not before Spin Doll sees it. Spin Doll rushes to place herself between Bee and their fake Cam. The two stare at each other, knowing something is about to happen. Agreeing that it's too dark and that they really do need some sleep, they all prepare for bed. Spin Doll places Bee in between herself and Bug, leaving Cam to fend for himself.

Cozzex, now knowing that Spin Doll is on to her, decides to make some hot water for them all. She pulls an herb from her pocket and dumps a little in Spin Doll's and Bug's cups. Cozzex knows the herb will knock them both out, making it easier for her to release them. Once the water is hot enough, Cozzex explains to the two that she's made them hot tea to help them relax and have a nice sleep. Bug excitedly gulps his down. Before Spin Doll can drink hers, Bee accidentally knocks the cup from her hand and spills it on the ground. A funny mist rises from the ground on contact. This now concerns Spin Doll even more. She couldn't have morning come sooner.

Spin Doll covers Bee up and closes her eyes, not really wanting to. Bug is fast asleep and snoring. The fake Cam closes his eyes and pretends to fall asleep. Cozzex knows once they're out, she'll be able to release all three. Patiently, she waits till all are asleep. Spin Doll is the last one to close her eyes. Once confirming they're out, Cozzex moves into place by sliding across the ground. She's unobservant that Spin Doll is still awake, only pretending to be asleep.

Spin Doll cracks her eyes slightly, revealing Cam standing over Bug with a long, short-handled dagger. Cozzex notices Spin Doll's eyes open, and immediately she dives on Spin Doll. Before Spin Doll can move, Cozzex holds her firmly from behind. Cozzex has one hand covering Spin Doll's mouth and the dagger slightly jabbed into her stomach. Spin Doll knows if she tries to move, Cozzex will run her through. With Cozzex pressed against her back and the dagger so close to releasing her light, Spin Doll is at her mercy.

Cozzex leans her mouth to Spin Doll's ear and whispers, "Look at them, sleeping like babies. If you try and struggle, it'll be the last you see of them. Do you understand?"

Spin Doll nods in agreement. Cozzex continues. "My plan worked just as I hoped. When Dak released Cam, it was only fitting I used his looks. Until your one thousand questions, everything was going along as planned. Now I think I have a new plan. I simply release you, followed by the baby. Then when Bug awakens, I just tell him Cam must have taken the baby. Then, when we get to Paradise and they let us in, I simply release the queen. Then it's game over for the good guys. If you decide to fight back, I'll simply release you all."

Tears roll down Spin Doll's face as she watches Bug and Bee sleep. She glances down at the ring on her finger. With no other option, Spin Doll grabs the handle of the dagger with both hands and plunges it into her stomach. She uses such force as it goes through her and into Cozzex's stomach. Feeling the dagger pierce her body as well, Cozzex's eyes widen at the pain.

Stunned, Cozzex yells, "What have you done?"

With a shaky voice, Spin Doll mumbles, "I will not let you take them. If I'm being released tonight, you're coming with me."

Cozzex gasps for air. With one final big gasp, Cozzex turns to blue goo and sinks into the ground. She has no bubble, showing she's pure evil. Spin Doll tries crawling to Bee and Bug, but her strength leaves her body just before she reaches them, and she rises into the sky, leaving just the dagger and her new wedding ring as her reminder. With no more pain she looks down at the sleeping two and blows a kiss. A sleeping Bug rubs his cheek as if he felt something.

Chapter 35

"When it's your turn to be the king, rip the wings off of angels, so nothing is above you." –Dak

Dak leaves Furrow's chambers to the faint sound of the final king's scream echoing down the tower's walls. When he reaches the door to the dungeon, he notices some blue goo trickling out of the bottom of it. A smile forms on his face as he reaches for the door handle. Swinging the door open leaves him facing hundreds of Octoros. The smile never leaves his face as he addresses the evil spiders.

"Ahh, my babies have finally arrived."

The Octoros spread out to reveal the final king's crown, lying on the dungeon floor. As did the two before it, the crown melted and became part of Dak's armlet, which begins to glimmer, and Dak can feel its power run through his veins.

Dak points down the tower hall toward the exit to the kingdom. He loudly commands the army of Octoros, "Now, my children, ravage the kingdom and fill your stomachs with all who remain."

The spiders do as they're told and head out into the kingdom. Dak watches every Octoro leave the dungeon, hearing the screams of the unfortunate followers who have stayed in the kingdom.

Dak walks to the cell that once held Jim. Seeing no bubble of blue goo, he knows Jim has, once again, escaped. Smiling, he looks down the dark dungeon and speaks to the emptiness.

"Jim, my guy. You have more lives than a cat. But eventually, my friend, you'll run out of them."

As he turns to leave, he notices the crushed cricket. Dak says to the cricket, "Oh, my friend Jim gave you a quick release. My children would have ripped you apart, making you feel everything, then they would've eaten you slowly. That old man still has a heart. It's a shame my babies will eat it." He steps on the squished cricket as he leaves.

Leaving the tower and stepping out into the kingdom, Dak watches his children chase down and devour every remaining follower one at a time. Within an hour, hundreds of innocent souls are released, leaving only Dak and his babies remaining. The Octoros surround Dak as they waited for their next orders.

Dak's looks change with every release. Dark blue veins take over his arms, legs, and face, making him much larger than he was. Now, standing close to seven feet tall and a hundred pounds heavier, he is no longer a person but a force to reckon with.

Standing there, admiring his takeover of the kingdom in a matter of minutes, he speaks to his children.

"My family, this is a new day. A day where I replace my father and make everyone fear me. I will take you across the Here and right up to the gates of pearl. We will take down the walls of Paradise, then take Paradise itself. I personally will release my mother, for it will be an honor for her to be released by the hands she raised. Then, and only then, will the Horizon be ours. Now, march toward Paradise and devour everything in your path. Leave nothing—end any signs of good. If you come across any angels, leave them for me. I must hear the sound their wings make as I rip them from their backs."

Dak points in the direction of Paradise and orders, "We take the Horizon now!"

The Octoros begin running, leaving nothing left in their way. Dak smiles, then begins following them as he whispers to himself, "Horizon, you're about to meet the real bad guy."

Chapter 36

"The Horizon is filled with many things. Evil shouldn't be one of them." –Dayne

Dayne sits on her throne overlooking Paradise. She simply can't get over the beauty in front of her. While lost in a daze, she is interrupted by Owl.

"My majesty, the twenty lost doors have been found and placed back in their original spots. All seem to be working and in good shape. They're a little smoky, but a little elbow grease and they'll be good as new. It seems as if everything is back to normal—except the baby, of course."

Dayne nods. "Thank you, but all is *not* normal. I feel as if something is coming that we may not be ready for. Please send for Hunter, Maverick, and Megan."

Owl bows as he backs away, then turns and runs off into Paradise.

Dayne falls back into her daze and starts to see Kannon's smile and his gaze in her eyes. Again, she's interrupted. This time it's the voice of an elderly woman.

"You know he's not gone, don't you?"

Dayne, confused by the lady's words, questions, "I'm sorry, I didn't see you standing there. Who's not gone?"

The old lady places her hand on Dayne's hand as she answers the queen. "Your husband. He's not gone. See, he's a giver. Givers don't go up into the stars. Sure, they're in bubbles, but when the babe is returned, they will burst their bubbles and crash back down into the Horizon. Givers get to return."

"Givers? What are Givers?"

The old lady chuckles. "When most come to the Horizon, they take their own lives to get here. But given a second chance here, they give up their lights to save someone else. So, they go from takers to givers. Life means so much more when you're a giver."

"How was my husband a giver?"

"He was given a light when he arrived. He gave up that light to save a loved one. He took swords to his chest to save his son. That makes him a giver. Givers get a chance to finish their stories. So, they get their light back." The lady hugs Dayne and hobbles off into the distance.

Dayne, still trying to process the old lady's words, has many thoughts race through her mind. *Is this true? Do givers return? Kannon might still be in the Horizon.* She knows she must find Bee. If Bee holds the chance to get her husband back, they need to find her sooner rather than later.

Owl returns with Hunter, Mav, and Meg, and stands at attention. Hunter approaches Dayne first.

"Dayne, did you ask for us?"

Dayne thanks Owl, then has him leave so she can talk to the three privately. Owl scurries off, not happy that he doesn't get to hear the conversation.

"Hunter, there may be a chance to save Kannon."

Hearing this makes Hunter all ears.

"The baby! The baby must be returned to Paradise. Kannon is a giver, and givers get to return to the Horizon once the baby has been returned."

Maverick joins the conversation. "Is this true, my queen?"

"I'm not sure, but for my husband's sake, I pray it is. Hunter, I need you three to go out and find that child. If you don't, I will."

Meg blurts out, "We'll leave immediately, my queen."

Hunter and the knights gather their weapons and approach the gates of pearl.

Owl runs between them and the gate, holding up his hands. "Whoa, whoa, whoa! Nobody leaves Paradise."

Dayne barks, "Owl, step aside, now!"

Owl steps aside, scared. The queen has never spoken to him in that tone.

The three warriors stand facing the gate, which begins to creak and crack as it opens.

Meg assures Dayne, "We will return with that baby."

"I know you will, Meg. I know you will. Godspeed, my friends."

As the three step through the gates, Dayne can hear Hunter say, "You know, I've done some crazy stuff before, but walking out of Paradise might top them all. Oh well; fuck it. You know what they say: you only live once."

Chapter 37

"For a dead man, he walks pretty damn fast." –Bob

Bee begins crying as Bug mumbles, "Spin Doll, baby."

With no answer and Bee getting louder, Bug raises his voice. "Spin Doll, for the love of God, please shut that baby up. It's not even morning."

Once again, he hears no reply, only Bee crying. "I swear to everything holy, if I have to get up, someone is getting their ass beat!"

But still, no one responds to his threat, and Bee cries louder. Bug sits up and rubs his eyes as he looks around. Spin Doll isn't lying in her spot, and Cam is no longer there as well. Bug stands and picks Bee up, slowly shaking her to calm her down. He looks all around at the little campsite they have. With no signs of Spin Doll or Cam, worry quickly settles into Bug's head. With Bee settled down, he begins to yell for his wife.

"Spin Doll! Spin Doll! Where are you? I need some help with Bee."

Still no answers come. Now panic sets in, and Bug frantically searches through the woods. After an hour of no response, Bug returns to their resting spot. He sits down, slowly shaking Bee as she sleeps. Millions of thoughts race through his mind. Then, Bug spots something on the ground. Reaching down, he picks up the wedding ring he gave Spin Doll, along with a dagger. Now fearing something has happened to her, he stands and immediately begins to run toward Paradise.

He tells Bee, "Since it was important to Spin Doll that we get you to this Paradise place, I'm taking you there. Then I will find my beautiful wife."

Bug runs until daylight. Finally, he must stop. His legs are exhausted and he needed to rest a bit. Holding Bee, he reaches into his bag and pulls out one of his old shirts that still has cake frosting on it from the big cake war at Dayne's house. Even though he's saving it, Bee needs it more. She smells so bad, he knows she'll give them away a mile down the road. After a quick change and gagging a few times, the mission is accomplished.

But before they get up from the changing spot, Bug can hear someone coming. Quickly, he finds a hiding spot. As the footsteps get closer, they sound heavier. Bug peeks out to see what it could be. His eyes grow large as he watches Hangman stomp past them. Bug whispers to himself, "The Hangman is still alive. How can that be? Char tore him apart."

Before Hangman is out of earshot, Bee lets out a giggle. Bug quickly covers her mouth. The Hangman stops and turns back toward them. He stands there trying to hear where the sound came from. Sweat beads roll down Bug's forehead as he tries to look through the high grass without being seen. No longer able to hear a noise, Hangman turns back around and continues on. A sigh of relief comes from Bug's chest. Knowing now how urgent getting Bee to Paradise is, he steps out from their hiding spot.

Lucky for them, Paradise is in a different direction than Hangman went. So off they walk, with Bee still in a giggly mood. Not far from the path, Bug notices two more figures heading in their direction. He's tired of hiding, so he places Bee on the ground and pulls out his bat. The closer the pair gets, the tighter Bug's grip gets on the bat. It isn't long before the men reach Bug. Bug pulls back his bat as the heavy man yells, "Whoa there, partner. We come in peace."

The skinny man follows. "Yeah, we come in peace."

Both men hold their hands up as they back away a little.

Bug forcefully demands, "What are you doing here? I want an answer now!"

The heavy guy extends his hand as he explains, "Name's Bob, this here is Spazz. We came here following the silent man."

Spazz adds, "Yeah, we watched that big dude crush a couple skulls. We need to stop him from hurting others."

Bug eases his grip a little, realizing the men seem to bring him no harm.

Bob continues. "Might I trouble you for your name and reason for standing in our way?"

Spazz adds, "Yeah, our way. You're standing in our way. Why?"

Bee giggles, giving away her hiding spot.

Bob loudly asks, "Is that a baby? Here in the Horizon?"

Spazz adds, "Oh, that's a baby. Why's a baby in the Horizon?"

Bug, still holding the bat, slowly reaches down and picks up Bee. Knowing he doesn't have to supply the pair with an answer, he explains. "This is Baby Bee. Sometimes he's a he, and other times she's a she. I don't know why, but my wife needed to bring this child to Paradise. Now that my wife is missing, it's my job to get Bee to her destination."

Bob chuckles. "So, you're a babysitter."

Spazz adds, "Yeah, he's babysitting with a bat."

That angers Bug. "I'm no babysitter. I'm a watcher. If you two don't make room for us to pass, I'll be watching your asses get a beat down."

Bob begins to lose his good-mood demeanor as he calmly states, "Now son, I'd suggest you lose that attitude before someone knocks it out of you. We mean you no harm. Shit, if you really need us to help you, we will. But never threaten us again. It's bad for my image to smack around a little guy like you."

Spazz once again follows. "Trust me, he'll smack a small dude."

Before Bug can answer, Bob adds, "So, Babe Ruth, do you want our help or not?"

Knowing how hard it would be to watch over and protect Bee, Bug agrees to the pair helping him. And after Bob and Spazz introduce themselves to Bee, the four begin their trek.

Chapter 38

"You ever feel so powerful that it seems unfair?" –Dak

With every last light released in the kingdom, Dak decides it is time to move on to bigger and better places. Standing in front of the hundreds of Octoros, Dak speaks to them.

"My babies, now we head for Paradise. I wonder if Mom will have dinner ready when we get there. We must eliminate Here and whatever light remains in it. We will accomplish what my father could not. Now we'll show the Horizon what power and fear look like. Come. Let me lead you to total dominance. Let's make the Horizon a place that punishes the weak—not gives them hope and lets them redeem themselves. Send every last light to the sky. Make them pay for giving up in their world. Weak shall no longer be welcomed here. Follow, as I lead us to Paradise and the end of the Horizon."

Dak begins marching as the Octoros follow in stride, releasing Shadows and villagers alike, filling the air with lights. Dak and his evil army clean the landscape of any living thing. Reaching the Knoll of Sight, which is the only hilltop that allows one to see for miles in any direction in the Here, Dak halts the army, spotting an image off in the distance heading for them. Surprised and a little angry, Dak wonders who would have the balls to approach him. The closer the image gets, the more recognizable the man becomes.

With a big smirk, Dak says, "Where have you been, my brother?"

The Hangman replies in a deep, slow voice, "Fucking dragons. Awful beasts. One caught me off guard and ripped me apart, scattering my body across the Horizon."

Dak informs Hangman that he has heard what had happened to him and that he has sent the Jokers to find him.

Hangman slowly replies, "They found me, but I now owe you two clowns."

"That's all right. I was done with them anyway. Now we march on to Paradise."

Hangman has other plans, though. "Sorry, but I'm going dragon hunting. Then I will join you and our sister as the power of three. You do know the only way to release Mom is to have the power of three impale her at the same time. I don't think Sis will be too interested in helping us. That reminds me: I sent the clown's sister to release our sis and the baby."

"I'm sure the bumbling fool will find some way to botch that," Dak answers.

The Hangman scowls. "Why would you try and release our sister? We need her to release our mother."

Dak rolls his eyes. "Knowing our goody-goody sister, if she's released, she did it saving another. When a savior gets released and all the lights head for the stars, the savior falls back to the Horizon, as if the Horizon wants to reward them."

"If that's the case, how will we release Mom? She gave up everything—Dad, us, her own world. Will she be returned back here?"

Dak informs his not-so-intelligent brother, "Mom is the key to ending it all. We release her, and the chain of return stops, along with those foolish doors. They'll be closed for good. Yes, Spin Doll will be returned to help us finish the Horizon once and for all. But only if we keep her precious Bug alive for insurance."

Both men now begin to laugh with evil expressions on their faces.

When their chuckles are finished, Dak reaches into both his pockets. He retrieves one item from each and holds them out in front of Hangman, with his fists clenched. Smiling, he tells Hangman to choose. The Hangman gestures toward Dak's right hand. Dak opens it, revealing IC, who looks awfully scared and weak. Then Dak opens his left hand, revealing Mim, who isn't moving and looks like she isn't long for the Horizon.

Hangman scoffs. "What do I want with a couple of star cleaners? They don't even look good enough to eat."

Dak pulls them back toward himself, once again clenching onto them. "We're not going to eat them." He turns and looks at IC, as he orders, "Now, little one, you're going to do us a favor. You're going to find us a dragon. If you don't succeed in returning with Char, I'll feed Mim to my children."

Knowing she doesn't have a choice, IC musters up enough strength and flies off into the distance.

Dak squishes Mim back into his pocket, and says to Hangman, "Now, you can help me, because that little star cleaner will bring Char right to us. It was awfully nice of the Jokers to catch these two little pests for me. I knew they'd come in handy."

Hangman smiles as he gestures toward the direction of Paradise. "Shall we then?"

Once again, the evil army begins to march.

Chapter 39

"Meeting a stranger who feels like a brother from a different mother."
–Bob

Reluctantly, Bug walks alongside Bob and Spazz while shaking Bee slightly to keep her calm. Trying to make small talk, Bug asks, "So, you two been friends for a while?"

Bob chuckles. "Since day one of getting here. It was kind of like we already knew each other, like we were friends even before we got here."

Spazz mumbles, "Brothers from different mothers."

Bug thinks it's amusing how Spazz always adds something to what Bob says.

Bob glances at Bug. "So, Bug, is this your baby?"

Spazz mumbles again. "Kinda look alike."

Bug quickly responds, "No, not at all! This baby is from Paradise. Someone kidnapped it, and I'm just being a good guy and returning it."

"So, you like just found it? Like, oh look, a baby."

Spazz must add, "Look, a baby under a bush."

Bug laughs. "No, my wife found the baby. Then a very bad guy stole it. Then my invisible friend stole it back and returned it to us. When I woke up, my wife and friend were gone. So, you see, I need to return this baby so I can go find my wife."

Confused, Bob asks, "So you lost your invisible friend? Was your wife invisible as well?"

Spazz mumbles, "How do you know you lost your invisible friend?"

Both guys look at Bug as if he's crazy.

Bug realizes how crazy that sounds, but it's true. To change the subject, Bug asks, "So is Bob your real name or is it short for something? Also, Spazz. Really!"

Bob chuckles. "Bob stands for Big Old Boy. As far as Spazz, well, just look at him. That boy's a couple of cans short of a six-pack. His elevator doesn't go all the way to the top. Shit. When they handed out brains, he got in the wrong line. Have you ever seen that commercial where they put the eggs in a pan and state, 'This is how your brain looks on drugs'? Yeah, Spazz was missing the frying pan. That boy's flapjack stack is smaller than everyone else's."

Spazz mumbles, "That boy's dumb as a stump, sure enough."

Bug laughs at the two making fun of themselves. He figures he'll add to it. "When I first saw you two walking toward me, you looked like the number ten."

Bob and Spazz immediately stop laughing. Bob says, "Are you calling me fat? You think I'm a zero?"

Spazz mumbles, "Well, you are fat. If you stopped walking, you'd still roll a few feet. I mean, you do have feet, or at least that's what we tell you."

Bob interrupts Spazz. "Listen, lightweight. I have to hold your hand when it's windy just so you don't blow away. Shit. Sometimes I lose you when you turn sideways. We can't have you walk through the woods, because if you accidentally rub against a branch, you'd start a fire. I have to fill your shoes with rocks so you can cross a stream."

Spazz interrupts Bob. "When we go out to eat, they just give you a chair at the buffet. You can't stand by a curb because police keep slapping tickets on you. Last time we went to the fair, people lined up by you thinking you were a bounce house."

They begin exchanging insults back and forth. "Remember when you got that bad sunburn on your face, and you couldn't walk down the road because cars kept stopping? How about that last solar eclipse you caused? Remember when that farmer offered you bucks to stand in his field and scare the birds away? Yeah, well, we appreciate you giving us the Grand Canyon on your one and only skydiving trip. What about the party we went to, and everyone tried hanging their coats on you? How about the time you were sunbathing on the beach and all those people tried to push you back into the water?"

Bug is laughing so hard that he has tears in his eyes. He begs them to stop.

Bob and Spazz both yell, "Truce!" at the same time as they laugh and hug each other. Now that they've stopped laughing and calmed down, the guys notice the gate to Paradise is just off in the distance.

Bug yells, "That's it!"

Bob replies, "Sure is. Ain't it beautiful?"

Spazz mumbles, "Looks like a bitch to climb over."

The men pick up their pace to a speed walk. Bob is the first to fall back a little, but he keeps a decent pace. Bug's eyes widen the closer they get. Finally, the three men and a baby stand in front of the gates.

Bug asks, "Do we just knock?"

Bob and Spazz shrug their shoulders since they have no idea. They've never seen Paradise before.

Bob whispers to Bug, "Go ahead and touch it."

Spazz mumbles, "That's what she said."

All three chuckle.

Bee opens his eyes, and, upon seeing the gates, lets out a loud squeal. The squeal is so loud it brings out a weird-looking guy standing on top of the gate. The guy yells, "Do not touch my gate!"

Bug yells back, "We have the baby! Let us in."

"You are small, but I wouldn't call you a baby."

Bob and Spazz giggle until the guy yells again. "Hey, baby, you have a huge Shadow following you, holding a spear!"

Bug laughs at that one, but Bob and Spazz do not.

Bob yells up at the man, "Are you going to let us in or not?"

"Keep your pants on, earth. I'll send the knights out."

Spazz chuckles and mumbles, "He called you earth."

Bob punches Spazz in the arm pretty hard. Spazz rubs his arm while giving Bob a dirty look.

After a few minutes, the gates begin to crack open, as the bright lights blind the men.

Chapter 40

"Well old friend, I guess it's true. All good things must come to an end." –Dak

As Dak and Hangman lead their army of Octoros across the lush green fields of Here, Hangman notices something off in the distance.

Dak, not being able to see what it is, asks, "Any idea what it is?"

Hangman replies, "Not really sure, but from here I'd say maybe a park bench."

Dak immediately thinks, *Could that be Jim?*

Eventually, when they get closer, they can see that it is indeed a park bench. Dak holds his right hand up, making the army stop in its tracks. He then tells Hangman to wait there while he checks it out. Slowly, he approaches the bench and sits down. To Hangman's surprise, Dak and the bench vanish. Dak is sure it's one of Jim's.

Patiently, he waits, but he doesn't have to wait long, Jim soon appears on the bench beside him. Dak smiles.

"Jim, my old friend, thanks for the assist on the king back there."

Jim, with his eyes looking toward the ground and his fingers locked on his lap, looks as if he's been beaten. In a calm, quiet voice, he replies, "Well, I guess this is it. I never was able to find my beloved Maggie."

Dak puts his arm around Jim's shoulders. "To think, you did all this to help me. Now look at you. A broken-down old man. No one would believe that such a little, crumpled old man could come up with such an elaborate plan. You know, you're the reason I'm where I am today. Everyone believed every word you said. You do look very trustworthy."

"I only did this for my Maggie. Don't for a minute think it was for anything else. I know you were lying about finding her. You promised that if I gave you the kingdom, you'd give me Maggie."

Dak yawns as he pats his mouth. "To be honest, I never really looked for her. I was your only shot, so I knew you would have no choice. Now, did I think you would deliver? No, but you surprised me. Bringing in these so-called warriors to help fool my father was priceless. You went and handpicked the best group of losers you could find. I would never have thought of using people who have already given up. Even my mom and dad thought they were losers who gave up as well. Now, with my father out of the picture, that only leaves mom and my sister left. Hopefully, our little Cozzex helped erase one of the two. It'll only be a few more hours before we reach mother. I can't wait for her to see how her boys grew up. I mean, my bro's a little worn out. But look at me; I've got the looks, the army, the leadership skills, and Paradise waiting for me in less than a day's walk. Now how about this, old buddy? I'm going to let you keep your light till I'm the total ruler of the Horizon. Mainly so you can see the destruction and devastation I leave behind. Once I gain control of Paradise and relieve my mother of her duties and light, I'll be back to release you and tie up any loose ends."

Jim can't believe the two monsters he made. The only thing he can do now is watch from a distance and pray he finds Maggie before the end.

Jim asks one more time, "What about Maggie?"

Dak shouts back at him, "Will you shut up about that old bitch for one minute? Maggie, Maggie, Maggie—she's not even here."

"What do you mean she's not here?"

Dak smirks. "I know I probably should have told you this earlier, but your precious Maggie is floating up around there somewhere." Dak points to the sky.

Jim looks up at all the floating released lights. With a shaky voice he questions, "What do you mean she's floating? How do you know this?"

Dak smirks again. "I met your Maggie like a couple of days after I met you. She told me who she was and asked if I'd seen you. Knowing that if you had her, you wouldn't help me, I released her. She didn't put up much of a fight. It was like I was doing you a favor. Really, you should be thanking me."

With every ounce of his body filled with anger, Jim reaches over and slaps Dak in the face.

Dak screams, "I will kill you, old man!"

"You already have!"

Dak stands up. "I will relieve you of that hand when I return. Then I will have the word Maggie tattooed on your forehead. That way people will ask why you have Maggie on your head. You can relive her memories over and over. Her name will haunt you forever." Dak walks away, leaving the broken old man to his lonely bench.

When Dak approaches Hangman, Hangman inquires, "Brother, why do you have a mark on your face?"

Dak barks back, "If I wanted you to know, I would've told you. Now get the fucking spiders marching again. I want to release mother before nightfall." Dak begins walking ahead of the army. The Hangman gives the march gesture, and the army is back on the move once again.

Chapter 41

"Little man, little man, let me come in before I blow your gate down."
–Bug

The men hold their hands out in front of them, trying to block the bright light from the gate. Bug yells, "Do you think maybe you could turn down the high beams?"

A dark figure appears from the light as the gate begins to close. Once closed, it takes the guys a few minutes to be able to see again. Eyes adjusted, Bug can see a young knight standing in front of them.

Bob sarcastically says, "We figured it'd be a good place to visit and lose our eyesight."

Spazz mumbles, "Yeah, I think I'm blind."

Not laughing, the knight responds, "If you've come to make jokes, this is not the place. You will be released."

Bug intervenes. "Whoa, buddy, nobody wants to be released. We're here to deliver this baby. But if it's an ass-whipping you're looking for, I can set this baby down, and we can settle your issue with us."

"The name's Willow, and trust me, it's more beneficial for you to continue holding the child."

Bob chirps in to ease the situation. "Willow it is. Can I call you Will? Well, Will, you see, we were told it was of utmost urgency that we get this baby to Paradise. So, if you could get someone from inside to give us some answers, we'll be on our way."

A voice responds from the top of the wall. "Hand your weapons to Willow, and we'll let you enter."

Everyone looks up to see Owl.

Bug quickly says, "Little man, how about you come down and take my weapons from me?"

Willow draws his sword. "That sounds like fun. I'll give it a try."

Bug hands Bee over to Bob and pulls his bat out from behind them. As the two begin to circle each other, Bug calmly states, "I'm about to turn you into a popsicle, boy."

Willow and Bug both swing their weapons, and the sword and the bat meet with a loud clank over their heads.

"Enough!" a voice from behind Bug demands.

Everyone turns to see a version of Dayne that Bug has never seen before.

Bug's eyes light up. "Dayne, is that really you?"

Dayne is trying not to smile but is happy to see her friend is safe. A little guy steps out from behind her and explains, "It is my queen to you, boy." She turns to Owl. "That'll be enough, Owl. This is my friend, Bug. Glad to see you well, Bug."

Bug delightfully replies, "Look at you, all queened up and looking good. Has Kannon seen you like this?" Then, almost as quickly as he says it, he remembers his friend is gone.

Trying to think of what to say next, Dayne orders, "Owl, take the babe into the gates to be examined."

Owl takes Bee from Bob's hands and scampers off into the gates. Dayne invites the three men into Paradise. Bug is hesitant, since he really must find Spin Doll. Bob and Spazz decline, even though they really want to see what's inside the gates. With a little persuading and an offer of food, the three follow Dayne through.

Once inside, the men's jaws drop. It is so beautiful and clean. It is a whole new world. Bug quickly notices the wall of doors that goes on forever.

"Hey, those look just like the doors in Fat Jack's cave."

Dayne informs him that they are doors that were stolen from Paradise but are now returned.

Puzzled, Bob asks, "What are so many doors needed for?"

Owl, who has returned empty-handed, explains, "Each door leads to someone's soul. When their life comes to an end, the queen sends an angel to retrieve their soul and bring them to the Here to be judged. If they live a nice long life, they are allowed in Paradise. If they pass before their time, they are placed in the Here to finish out their time. But if they take their life, they go to the kingdom and must amend for their turn to be placed in the Here. Not everyone sent to the kingdom makes it to Paradise. Once you enter Paradise, the only place left to go is up there as a star. Stars are the ultimate reward." Everyone is silent as they stare at Owl pointing at the sky.

Bob interestedly inquires, "By any chance do you know which one might be mine?"

Owl snaps back, "If we did, it wouldn't benefit us to show you."

Bug explains to Dayne and some of the knights how Dak released them all and wanted to take over all of the Horizon. He also explains how he needs to go find Spin Doll. Dayne offers the knights' service, as Willow and Russ offer themselves. Bug gladly accepts their help, along with Bob and Spazz who aren't leaving his side.

Dayne knows they must leave soon, so she has food quickly prepared. The five eat till they're full and then head for the gate. Just as they begin to open the gate, a familiar voice surprises the five warriors.

Chapter 42

"Just when you think you know someone, bang—you don't." –Bug

"Hey, is that how we treat friends? What, we no longer say hi to each other?" Hunter's familiar voice bellows out.

Bug smiles as he turns to greet his friend. The two embrace as Hunter picks Bug off the ground.

"Put me down. Put me down!" Bug tries not to be seen by the rest.

Hunter returns him to the ground, with a huge smile on his face. The two picked up where they left off.

"When did you get here?" Bug shouts.

"A few days ago. This place is nice, but you wouldn't want to live here. Everything is done for you. You just sit here and exist. So, where are we going?"

Bug smiles, happy his friend is coming with them. He turns toward the rest of the group. "Let me introduce you to Bob and Spazz."

Before Bug can say another word, Bob blurts out, "If it isn't our old flamboyant friend, Hunter."

"Gentlemen, it's been a while," Hunter addresses the two warriors.

Bug looks at Bob and Spazz. "You know each other?"

"Know each other? Not only do we know each other, but Hunter was the first one we met here. Never thought we'd be friends, but here we are."

"Why wouldn't you be friends? Because Hunter's a badass and you two not so much?"

Hunter jumps in. "Bob and Spazz can handle themselves. I've personally watched them release a group of twenty or so Shadows."

Dayne, surprised to see that her men have not made it that far asks, "You've returned so soon?"

Hunter smiles. "My queen, we noticed the gentlemen approaching the gate. We had to make sure it was safe for you and Paradise. Once I noticed who it was, we raced back to see if they'd be up for an adventure."

Bug, trying to make sense of it all, asks Spazz, "So you're surprised that you're friends, why?"

Spazz answers, "You know."

Bug looks at him with a blank stare, still puzzled.

Bob adds, "Because of the way Hunter is."

Bug, now even more puzzled, has absolutely no idea where this is heading. "The way he is. What the hell does that mean—the way he is?"

Hunter butts in. "We really should be going. We need to find the rest of our friends. Now that you've returned the baby and made our job easier, we can go save some lost souls and bring them back here."

Bug puts his hand up to stop Hunter as he questions Bob again. "What do you mean, the way he is?"

Bob begins to fumble his words. "You know… the way he is."

Spazz mumbles, "Big boy just stuck his foot in his mouth."

Bug stands firm, waiting for an answer. Everyone goes quiet as they stare at each other. Hunter reaches over and grabs Bug's shoulder. "Let's go. It's really nothing important."

Bug pulls his shoulder away and demands, "We're not going anywhere. Not until Bob explains the way you are statement."

Bob, trying to talk his way out of it, replies, "I didn't mean anything. It was a joke."

Bug refuses to budge.

Finally, Hunter blurts out, "He meant because I'm gay. But he was joking."

Bug laughs. "Because you're gay? They think you're gay?"

"Bug, I *am* gay. I always have been," Hunter explains.

Bug stands there with his mouth gaping open. For the first time, he's speechless. Millions of thoughts roll through his mind. He slowly turns and walks out, and the group quietly follows him.

As the gates close, Owl runs up to Dayne. "My queen, the baby is fully healthy. That means it can be sent back to its place in the sky. All the stars and bubbles can go to their final resting place. Everything will be returned to normal."

Dayne sighs with relief. "All will be returned except those who sacrificed their lights for someone else. They'll be returned to us."

Owl begins to walk away, yelling, "Prepare the baby for its return! Let's get everything ready for the ceremony."

Dayne is relieved to get things back as they were before. But she has a strange feeling that everything isn't going to go smoothly. She goes to her loft to prepare for the ceremony and to look over the wall, as her friends depart Paradise and head out into the Here.

Chapter 43

"Heads are going to roll with the return of the king." –Dayne

Once the small group of warriors is out of sight, Dayne dresses for Baby Bee's send-off. In a beautiful light purple dress, she stares at herself in the mirror. Still not 100% sure why she was chosen as Queen of Paradise, she lets her mind wander. *Ok Dayne, you sit here all alone. You lost Kannon, the only love of your life.* The more she thinks of Kannon, the more she wonders how long she'll have to rule Paradise all alone. Tears fill her eyes and then begin running down her face. She feels she should have been released alongside him, so neither of them would have to go on without the other. Then she thinks, *They all think you're the lucky one. Little do they know, you are the biggest loser.*

A knock comes at her door, interrupting her thoughts.

Owl calls out, "My queen, we are ready for you. Everyone is patiently waiting in the garden."

"Be right there." Wiping the tears away, she opens the door and heads to the garden. Approaching the garden, she sees Baby Bee playing in the center of many onlookers. The crowd parts to let the queen enter.

Reaching the baby, Owl hands her a scroll. "My queen, once you read this aloud, the baby will take its place in the sky only if he thinks you're true to the words."

Dayne unrolls the paper, and before she reads it, she bends down and kisses Bee on the forehead. Everyone is silent as Dayne begins to read.

"You were brought to us because something wasn't right. We need you to return and give us back our night. When you fell, the stars followed you down. We fought demons and nightmares till they were all found. Now rise and reclaim your space in the sky so the ones down here can wish with their eyes. Watch over all those who have earned the right to die so they can join you in filling the new night sky. For the stars are not given; they are earned. May you forever stay above us and never return. Now light up the sky with all my lost friends so we can rejoice that their story had a happy end."

Baby Bee begins to giggle as she floats up toward the sky. The higher she rises, the brighter she becomes, until she takes her rightful form as the biggest and brightest star in the sky. Once she is where she belongs, the bubbles all begin to rise. One by one they take their spots in the sky. The entire sky fills with stars, and Dayne wonders which one is Kannon. The familiar tears begin to fill her eyes once more. Leaving the crowd, she returns to her loft high above Paradise to watch the spectacle on her own.

Hunter tries to talk to Bug, but Bug just turns away from him and continues watching the sky. Bug prays none of the rising lights are his beautiful wife's light.

* * *

Miles away, Dak, Hangman, and the army of Octoros watch as so many orbs take the shapes of stars. The smile widens on Dak's face as he wonders which one is his father. He turns toward Hangman.

"Even though Dad is up there alone, he got everything he deserved. Soon, we'll send mom to join him. Then they can watch over our reign of terror as we punch every last soul that had given up in their world. Oh, how we'll make them pay."

Both men begin to laugh.

The warriors, who have already made camp for the night, all lie on their backs and watch the most beautiful light show they have ever had the pleasure of watching. They point out certain stars, wondering if they might have been friends they had known.

Chapter 44

"Welcome back, my friend. I knew this wasn't the end." –Hunter

"Damn it! Cozzex must have failed me. The baby was returned to the sky!" Dak shouts.

"Who cares? They'll all be up there soon enough." The Hangman calms Dak down a bit. "Besides, in a couple of days, we'll be the only ones to look at the stars. You can have Paradise, and I'll take the kingdom."

His brother's words are reassuring to Dak.

Dak lies on his back and begins counting the stars as they go into the sky. He wonders how many of them he personally sent up there. Feeling tired, he closes his eyes for a quick nap. But that is short-lived as his pocket begins to move, which startles him. Reaching down, he pulls Mim out. She looks like she has very little light left.

"I totally forgot about you. Your sister better deliver, or I'll let Hangman eat you."

Mim barely cracks her eyes open. The Hangman adds, "I'm not Fat Jack. That thing looks awful. It probably tastes even worse. Why don't you just toss it to the Octoros? Give them something to play with."

Both men laugh, and Dak agrees and tosses Mim toward a small group of Octoros. To their surprise, Mim has been leading them on a little more than they thought. Before reaching the group, Mim takes flight and heads toward Paradise. Dak jumps up quickly in an attempt to grab her but misses. Turning to order the Octoros to catch her, he's interrupted by a loud BOOM. It came from behind the Octoros, perhaps the kingdom. Taking his mind off Mim, he orders three of the Octoros to go check it out. As they race off, he turns and can no longer see Mim. Now angry and frustrated, he can no longer sleep.

Hangman laughs at his brother. "Ahh, let's not worry about that little bug. She barely has a light left. Shit, she won't make it half a mile before she joins the rest of the stars. As for that boom, it was probably the last tower collapsing. Get some rest. We have a Horizon to conquer tomorrow."

* * *

The noise is so loud that Bug and the crew hear it as well. Mav points toward the kingdom. "It sounded as if it came from that direction."

Bug complains, "Well, it looks like we won't be sleeping tonight."

Hunter takes this as a chance to get Bug talking. "Since we can't sleep, maybe we should have a talk. Bug, I understand if you're mad because I'm gay."

"You think I'm mad and not talking to you because you're gay? Dude, I don't care if you're black, brown, white, blue, or yellow. I don't care if you like men, women, or farm animals. I'm mad because we were supposed to be best friends. But, obviously, we're not because you didn't feel the need to share this with me, but you can with Bob and Spazz."

"No, it's not like that. When you met me, you thought I was a badass tough guy. I thought if I told you guys I was gay, you'd think of me as a liability."

Bug scrunches his face. "A liability? You took on the Beast twice. Man, I looked up to you like a brother."

Hunter looks down at the ground, ashamed. He begins to tell Bug his story. "My real story is I was a very popular singer. I filled stadiums every night. My boyfriend would never come and watch me. He thought if someone found out I was gay, it would ruin my career. Finally, I talked him into attending the last concert of the mini tour. I got him in the front row, just off to the side. Little did he know that I was going to come out and ask him to marry me.

"That night was perfect. The crowd was so into it. Every time I looked toward my boyfriend, he would smile and give me a slight wave while dancing to my music. With my most popular song left, I knew that was the moment. I had the stagehands bring up the lights, and my band stopped playing. Then, with thousands listening, I came out to the world. A hush filled the crowd, and my boyfriend's looked as if he had just seen a ghost. Before I could introduce him and propose, they turned on me. They began throwing things at me and booing. When I turned to my boyfriend, he was booing and yelling just like the crowd. I ran off the stage and jumped into the nearest car with keys. I drove off, almost unable to see with tear-filled eyes. I lost my career and my love in a matter of minutes. Suddenly, I missed a turn, not being able to see through the tears, and went over an embankment."

Bug quickly hugs his friend, as do Bob and Spazz. Soon the knights join the hug as well.

But the hug doesn't last long because another sound is heard much closer. They quickly draw their weapons and head for the sound. When they approach the area, they find an indentation in the ground surrounded by a black burnt outline. In the middle of the burnt area lies a medium-built young man.

Bug and Hunter approach the man. "Buddy, are you alright?"

When the man rolls over, to Bug and Hunter's surprise, they see it's Dillo.

Bug yells as he runs to help his old friend up. "Dillo, is that really you?"

Dillo smiles, happy to see his old friends. "Hunter and Doug—is that you?"

Hunter laughs because he knows Dillo is just busting Bug's balls.

While helping Dillo out of the hole he made, the warriors hear two more booms off in the distance. Instantly, the group gathers Dillo and their supplies and heads off to the nearest boom they've heard.

Chapter 45

"This is the part of our journey where the shit hits the fan." –Spazz

The three Octoros approach the kingdom, busting through what wall is left. They see a figure standing in a burnt hole. Their thoughts are to immediately attack and destroy him. With his tattered, ripped clothes, the man stands and acknowledges his soon-to-be attackers. When he turns toward the attacking spiders, the moonlight reveals a much meaner-looking Kannon.

The first Octoro leaps toward him as Kannon places a well-aimed shot through most of the spider's abdomen. The other two stop in their tracks. Before they can turn and run, Kannon dispenses with another one. The third rushes out of distance, only to be heard squealing in pain.

A few seconds later, Colt appears standing in front of Kannon covered in blue goo.

Wiping off her face, she says, "Kannon, is that you? How'd we get back here? And where are the others?"

Kannon brushes the dirt and goo from his shoulders, never looking up at Colt.

Colt nervously asks again, "Kannon, are you alright? You seem different. Where is everyone else?"

Kannon looks up with the evilest of faces and slowly demands, "Go! Go tell them that Daddy is home!"

Colt, backing up, quickly turns and is gone from sight.

Kannon looks at his destroyed kingdom. The only thing left standing is one tower. His already angry body fills with even more anger as he lets out a hideous scream that can be heard through the entire Horizon. Stepping out from his landing spot, Kannon mumbles to himself, "Heads are gonna roll. I'm about to fill the sky with stars. You wanted the real Kannon—you've got him! Someone forgot this is my Horizon!"

* * *

Dak jumps to his feet, hearing the scream. He yells to Hangman, "What the fuck was that?"

The Hangman smiles. "Dad's home." The Hangman clenches his fist and turns back toward the kingdom and begins walking.

Dak yells, "Where are you going? Paradise is the other way!"

The Hangman speaks just loud enough for Dak to hear. "I'm going to finish the job you couldn't. You go say hi to Mom. I'll take care of the pop."

Dak nervously calls over one of the Octoros. "My brother has lost his mind. I need you to go get the monsters. Bring them both. We need the gate breakers. Go now! Be quick!"

The Octoro runs off into the darkness.

* * *

Bug and Hunter are so happy to have their friend back. Knowing the battle is coming, they'll need all the help they can get. Then the scream reaches their ears, sending some of the warriors into a panic.

"What the hell was that?" Bug asks.

Hunter and the group shrug their shoulders.

Dillo whispers, "I take it I'm not the only one to return."

Before they can say something else, Colt appears in front of them, breathing heavily.

Hunter bursts out, "Colt, you're back as well! It is so good to see you, baby girl."

Bug, Hunter, and Dillo rush to her. Bug hands her water. She quickly drinks her fill, then tries to speak.

"Dak is leading a whole army of Octoros toward Paradise. He's not the Dak we thought he was. There's more. The Hangman is with him."

Hunter looks at her in shock. "The Hangman is with him? Char tore him limb from limb."

Colt shakes her head. "I'm telling you it is him. But he was heading toward the kingdom in the opposite direction."

Bob jumps in. "Little lady, what's the Octoro you mentioned?"

Bug explains, "They're giant spiders with bull horns on their heads."

Dillo begins to panic. "No, I must go home. I can't fight without my shell. I don't want to die again. Hunter, please take me home."

Hunter hugs Dillo to calm him down.

Bob and Spazz both whisper to Bug, "What does he mean, his shell?"

Bug explains to them about Dillo's grandpa's armadillo shell that he gave Dillo to wear for protection. He explains how, with the shell on, Dillo felt unstoppable.

Hunter says, "Dillo, your shell was destroyed in the battle with the Beast. We no longer have it."

Dillo collapses to the ground in fear.

Bob and Spazz have their own little conversation, which leads Bob to call Colt over to their private meeting. Colt takes off into the darkness. Mav quickly insists on being told what was said to Colt to make her leave. Bob tells the group to hold their horses; she'll be returning shortly. Bug can't wait around. One of those booms came from the direction he last saw Spin Doll. Hunter sends Mav and Meg with Bug, as the rest await Colt's return. The three head off into the darkness.

Hunter orders Russell to head back to Paradise and inform the queen of Dak and his army of monsters. Russ runs off in the darkness in the opposite direction of Bug's group. Hunter, Bob, and Spazz try to console Dillo until Colt's return.

After about a forty-minute wait, Colt returns holding a giant crab shell. Bob laughs.

Colt holds the shell out. "I know this isn't an armadillo shell, but this crab shell might even be stronger. I found it one day on my beach and had it in my collection. It's yours, Dillo, if you want it. Hope it protects you better than its previous owner."

A huge smile enters Dillo's face as he jumps up and grabs the shell from Colt. It's a little tighter fit, but Dillo gets the crab shell on. Dillo excitedly screams, "It fits! It's smoother and shinier. Go ahead.

Someone punch me in the stomach."

Spazz gives Dillo a good punch to the gut. Dillo doesn't even move as Spazz shakes his hand in pain.

Hunter asks Dillo, "You good to fight now?"

"Bring on those chickens and goats. Crab Man is here."

Everyone laughs as they head in Bug's direction.

Bob leans over to Colt. "Thank you, little lady. You're welcome to use my beach whenever you want."

Colt laughs and hugs Bob. Colt smiles at Hunter and informs him, "I like these two; great addition to an already great family."

Chapter 46

"A father's love goes beyond this world." –Kannon

Kannon stands at the top of the hill overlooking the kingdom that was once his world, the crumbled walls and emptiness where small shops once stood—three of the four towers no longer standing. He would've given his boys everything. Why would they destroy it all? His anger is all over the place. Should he seek revenge or rebuild what's left?

Kannon softly speaks in the darkness. "What kind of world is this? It brings my wife and me here. It hands us three kids that aren't ours and tells us it's our responsibility. It hands me darkness and in return gives my wife the light. In between us, it fills in with Here. Why give us a family when they bring us here, then split us? I wanted to spend my whole life with my beautiful wife, Dayne. Now we stand in tower windows and stare at each other because good and evil cannot exist in the same place. I thought if we left our world and came here, we could finally be together. But this world is just as cruel as our past one."

Kannon hears clapping from behind as he turns to see Hangman walking toward him.

"Always such a showman. Poor me. Poor Kannon." The Hangman's voice drips with sarcasm.

"Why are you here, Son?" Kanon speaks in a low tone.

"Surprised to see me, Dad? You put your poor boy in a hole, covering him with cement in an old building, never to escape. Well, to my surprise, my caring brother found me and helped me out. So now I owe him. I'll erase you and Mom and maybe Sis for him. I'll give him the power he seeks… for a little while, at least. Then he'll join you up there." Pointing toward the stars, Hangman smiles at Kannon.

Anger can no longer fit in Kannon's body as he draws his sword and cocks his cannon.

"Aw, does Daddy want to play?"

"If you step toward me, you never will again," Kanon warns him.

Hangman smiles as he steps toward Kannon. "Yeah, I don't think I'll let you do that again."

The two charge each other. Kannon fires first, taking a chunk out of his son's arm. Before reaching his son, the piece of arm heals. The two collide, knocking them both to the ground. They tumble and roll down the hillside, getting in what swings and shots they can. By the time they reach the bottom, they're both covered in blood.

This world has never seen such hatred. One after another, the two exchange blows. Hangman works his way to his father's backside, getting a headlock on him. Kannon struggles, trying to relieve Hangman's grip.

"I've waited years for this day. My only regret is that Mom can't watch your end. Dad, your story is different from most. You never hear of evil ending evil." Hangman tightens his grip.

Kannon's face is dark red, but Hangman can't tell if it's from lack of air or anger. Kannon drops to one knee, throwing over an unsuspecting Hangman. Before his son can stand, Kannon slams his knees into his face, blinding Hangman for a few seconds. When Hangman gains his whereabouts, he finds his father standing over him with a cannon in his face. Kannon knows he can end his son's light with one pull of the trigger.

"Son, I never wanted it to end this way. But I can't let you hurt your mother."

Hangman's face turns to sadness as he begins to beg his father. "Daddy, don't do it. For years I lay in that cement tomb wondering how my parents could do that to their child. You think I want to be like this? When evil is all that you know, evil is all that you do. You think I don't love my mom? My brother was the first one to show me compassion and what little love there is. Maybe you should release me and save this world, because if you don't, I will destroy it. Go ahead—be a hero!"

Kannon can't believe this is the first time he's seen his son so weak and vulnerable. Slowly he lowers his cannon and backs off his son. Thoughts race through his head. *How could you do this to your son? What kind of monster are you?*

Next thing Kannon knows, he's on his back with his son standing over top of him. "I'm sorry, I'm sorry I have such a weak father. You make me sick to be your child. I can't believe you actually thought I had a heart. Well, Dad, time to go." Hangman raises Kannon's sword. But before he can bring the sword down, he hears a screech off in the distance. Quickly he stumbles backward, softly saying, *"Dragon."*

Kannon crawls away from his son, seeing the flames in his eyes.

Kannon can't believe what his son is doing. He hasn't heard anything or known what's happening in his head. His son is in a bad place. Not knowing how to help him, Kannon leaves him to deal with his demons. Quickly, Kannon enters the darkness toward Paradise.

Even though he has widened the ground between himself and his son, he can hear Hangman yelling into the darkness, "Damn you, dragon! Show yourself! I'm right here!"

Chapter 47

"When you see a war coming, a war is what you prepare for."
–Dayne

Meanwhile, with about a mile from where Bug last saw Spin Doll, he begins to question Hunter to make the walk seem quicker. "So, have you been gay long?"

Hunter smiles at Bug's stupid question. "Pretty much all my life."

"So, this whole time in the Horizon, you've been gay?"

Hunter nods, wondering where his friend is going with these questions.

"Now that makes sense why you always wanted me to walk in front of you. You were checking out my ass."

Bob laughs. "What ass? You're a hundred and forty pounds soaking wet. You don't have an ass. Just a crack in your back."

Everyone laughs out loud, making Bug a little mad.

"I've been told I'm cute. Compared to this group, I'm a model," Bug snots back.

Spazz interjects. "Hundred and forty pounds if he was holding twenty pounds of rocks."

Bug, furious, stops dead and turns toward Bob and Spazz. "You know, you two seem to run your mouths quite a bit. What brought you to the Horizon? I know it wasn't exercise."

Bob smiles, not taking little Bug seriously. "Boy, listen, I used to be one of those slap fighters. You know. I would slap a guy, and if he could take it, he'd slap me back. We'd take turns until one of us couldn't stand. I was champ for my weight class. Day after day, people would want my belt. I was in so many bouts, the doctors recommended I stop for a while. But a champ doesn't quit. One night, I guess this big guy caught me good. I collapsed, and they couldn't revive me. The next thing I know, I'm here on my back. As far as Spazz goes, drug overdose."

Bug is caught off guard with their answer, so he turns back toward Hunter. "So, back to watching my ass."

Hunter laughs. "Not in a million years."

Bug is kind of insulted. "Yeah, okay, think what you want, but I know I'm hot. If this Horizon had a calendar of hot guys, I'd be like five different months. That's all I'm saying."

Mav speaks up. "Are we almost there yet? We're getting too far from Paradise."

But before anyone can answer, they stumble on an indent in the ground with a burnt ring around it—just like Dillo's. They begin to inspect the burnt spot when they hear a scream coming from the woods.

With weapons drawn, they ran toward the sound. On the other side of the wooded area, they find Spin Doll surrounded by Shadows and a couple large demon dogs. Mav and Meg have only heard about these demented, large, destructive dogs that feed on lights. Till now, they thought they were only stories.

Colt disappears into the woods. With bat charged up, Bug leads the charge as the rest follow. More Shadows and dogs come from the woods. Bob, face-to-face with a demon dog, reaches out and slaps the teeth out of the dog's mouth, while Spazz runs it through with his spear. Mav and Meg release Shadow after Shadow as they continue to pour out of the woods. Hunter is fighting off two demon dogs at once, which keeps him from switching his pool stick to his guns. Bug quickly makes it to Spin Doll, grabbing her around the waist. Leading her behind the warriors, he wonders why she isn't fighting back.

Slowly, the warriors hold off the attack, while making their way back through the woods to the clearing. Evan more Shadows pour out of the tree line. The warriors wonder if they'll ever stop. Finally able to thin out the attackers, the trees begin to break and tumble to the ground. Before they know it, a giant demon dog stands in front of them. The warriors stand in a line, not backing away from the giant dog. Mav swallows hard as Dillo steps in front of the group. With drool dripping from its jaws and bright red eyes, the dog stands in front of the group looking for the weakest.

"Sit! I said, sit!"

The warriors can't believe the balls Dillo has facing the deadly dog. The dog leans toward Dillo, almost face-to-face. Dillo can feel the dog's breath hit him in the face. In a demanding tone, he orders the dog again.

"I said sit. I won't tell you again. Sit!"

The demon dog draws his head back, then lunges toward Dillo. With a huge explosion, all that's left of the dog is its four paws. Nothing else. The warriors turn to see Kannon and Colt standing off in the distance. Kannon's cannon is smoking.

"When he tells you to sit, you fucking sit."

Dillo smiles. "About time."

"Ladies and gentlemen, I give you Kannon."

Bob leans over to Mav and Meg. "I'm glad he's on our side."

The knights draw their weapons towards Kannon. Mav yells, "Back evil king, or I will slay you!"

Kanon whispers loud enough for Mav to hear. "Not tonight, knight. Lower your sword or eat it. I'm not the guy you want to talk to that way."

Hunter and Bug jump between the two and calm the situation.

Chapter 48

"A lost love found is never the same." –Bug

The morning sun crests over Paradise as angels fill the top of the Paradise wall. All armed and ready to sacrifice their lights for it.

Dayne, not taking her eye off the ridge in the distance, says, "My angels, I appreciate your loyalty. But if my life is what they crave, and it will save Paradise, I will surrender to save your lights."

"My queen. We've lost you once; it will not happen again. I assure you of this."

No more words are spoken.

An hour passes, and still, every angel holds its post. Suddenly, a figure appears on the ridge. It seems as if the figure is alone. A few minutes later, a second figure appears alongside the first. Dayne pulls a long eye from her pocket. She holds it up to her eye and points at the figures. The long eye reveals the two figures to be Dak and Hangman.

"Evil has finally reached the gates of Paradise. If they breach our gates, destroy the doors. Make me this promise."

All the angels bow in acknowledgment of Dayne's words.

Then Dayne pulls the long eye up to her eye once again. This time the ridge is completely covered as far as she can see. Octoros, demon dogs, and Shadows fill the landscape. Then she watches as the army of monsters begins to move apart, leaving five large openings. The smile on Dak's face is large enough to see as he holds up one arm. It looks as if he's directing something. Then simultaneously the five gaps are filled with what looks like giant heads, as the ridge reveals five beasts. Dayne's face loses all expression as she can feel the ground shake with every step the beasts take. Dak lowers his arm as the army begins to charge toward Paradise.

Dayne addresses the angels once again. "I'm sorry. I'm sorry about everything. Owl, the doors. Destroy them all." Before any of them can respond, Dayne jumps off the wall and charges the oncoming army. Many angels follow her lead and leap to what is for sure their deaths.

Owl runs to the doors and begins smashing them one at a time. Russell freezes. He can't move. Suddenly, Mim appears from nowhere and lands on his shoulder. She looks much better than when she arrived.

Mim whispers in Russ' ear, "It's alright to be scared. But don't worry, because they're here." Mim points to the sky behind them. The sky is dark and looks as if it's coming toward them.

When the dark sky finally reaches them, Russell can see it's more than a hundred dragons, and Char is leading them. Time seems to slow down as the dragons fly over Paradise and Dayne's army. Dayne never looks up. She just knows Mimic came through for her once again.

Dak's eyes light up as Hangman yells, "Kill the fucking dragons! I told you, brother, today we battle. Tomorrow is the day we celebrate."

Kannon, leading the group, sends Colt up ahead to see why the sky is so dark in the distance. It looks as if the daylight and night sky are fighting for territory.

Bug is more concerned as to why Spin Doll doesn't fight back. He stops and pulls her aside. "Spin Doll are you alright? Why didn't you fight back there?"

"If I fight back and lose, I will never get released from the cage. No, it is better to do as they say. That way I won't get put back in the cage."

"What cage? I rescued you from the cage months ago. I promised you they would never cage you again. Besides, what kind of husband would I be if I didn't protect my wife?"

Spin Doll is puzzled. "Husband? I'm not married. I'm sorry, but I don't really know who you are."

"We're married. You really don't know who I am?"

Spin Doll shakes her head. "Since I woke up in the burnt circle, I don't remember anything."

"You don't remember any of us? Battling all the Shadows, the Jokers, the Beast, or witch? Nothing? The Jokers are the ones who put you in the cage."

Spin Doll shakes her head. "No, my brother, Dak, placed me in the cage. He told me that Mom and Dad put our brother in a tomb, and I was to be locked up. He was only allowed out if he watched over us."

"So, who are your mother and father?" Bug is confused and upset.

"Kevin Allen Nowles is my father, and Debra Ann Yarlow-Nowles is my mother."

Bug thinks for a moment, then it hits him. "So your dad's initials are KAN and your mom's is DAYN."

"Yeah, why?"

Bug laughs. "KAN and DAYN. Kannon and Dayne are your parents?"

Spin Doll's face drops as she realizes Bug is right. This seems to jog her memory a little, as he asks about other parts she remembers.

"Why were you in the burnt circle? Only the ones who passed returned that way. Also, what happened to Cam?" Bug doesn't understand.

Once he mentions Cam, everything floods back into her mind. She immediately hugs Bug with tears in her eyes. She tells him the whole story about how Cozzex was Cam and how she took her life to save Bug and the baby. Then she quickly asks Bug how Bee is. Bug points to the sky—to the brightest star—and explains that is Bee. Spin Doll asks for her ring back, and Bug can't get it out of his pocket and back on her finger fast enough. Everything is good again for the happy couple.

Suddenly, a much louder boom rings out. Thinking it's the war, the warriors begin to sprint.

Chapter 49

"Hey, hey, the gang's all here. After this battle, we better have beer."
–Bob

Both armies halt a hundred yards apart and size each other up. Dayne breaks the silence first. "Dak, why are you doing this? I order you, as your mother, to end this before it starts."

Dak chuckles. "Oh man, this has already started. You remember your long-lost son, Hangman."

"You brought dragons! Don't you remember I slaughtered all the dragons? That's why you placed me in that tomb. This will be déjà vu." Char's eyes peer at Hangman, as he is her only target.

"Where are your warriors? Did they all run and hide? I was looking forward so much to releasing them. Ah, well, why don't you save us all the trouble and hand me the keys to the gate?" Dak suggests smugly.

"I will give you something, but it won't be the key. I was thinking maybe introducing you to my releaser."

Dak, still smiling, says, "Let me introduce you, too. Oh wait. You met the Beast before. I thought maybe five of them were overkill. But since I have the money and the time, why not splurge? Oh yeah, Hangman here went and visited Dad. He sends his regards and really wishes he could have made it."

"I can speak for myself. Sorry, dear. I had to help our daughter pick out a dog."

Both Dayne's and Dak's faces drop in surprise when Kanon appears.

"Sis, glad you weren't tied up. You get to see your parents for the last time. It's like a family reunion. Don't worry. We won't release you. You'll be our pet." Dak laughs and nudges Hangman.

Bug just can't let that fly. "Dak, just to let you know, I'm going to be the one to release you."

Dak laughs. "Little piece of shit, you won't survive the first five minutes. Why are you still here? Really, out of all the warriors, you're still here? I'll clean my boots with your bat. And I'll make my sis watch."

Before any more can be spoken from the two sides, the ground begins to slightly tremble every three seconds. Both sides look around to see what's causing the disturbance. Soon, behind Dayne's army comes a large figure.

It's Hoss. He's back.

"What's this? He didn't surrender his light for others. What magic is this?"

Dayne smirks. "Oh, but he did. Back in his world, he saved children from a burning building. The prophecy doesn't fall only on the Horizon."

Hoss stops behind the line of angels and dragons. "Hey, hey, the gang's all here. Have you ever heard of the story of how one Hoss defeated five beasts? Well, let me begin."

All hell breaks loose as both armies charge into a heap of blood, goo, and clashing weapons. This is the beginning of a war that will have a winner.

Off in the distance—way up on a hill—Jim sits on his bench observing the whole thing.

"Well, this is all because of me. I wanted my Maggie more than the world. I'm the cause of the Horizon destruction. If I can't sit and stare at the Horizon with my beautiful wife, then no one shall. Oh Maggie, things would've been so different if I could have found you. I made a promise to give you the world. If I don't have you, I don't need this or any world."

Jim slides back and watches as lights rise to the stars.

Chapter 50

"The most feared thing by angry people is love." –Dillo

Completely outnumbered, the warriors fight with every ounce of energy they have. Kannon fires round after round, sending good and bad flying in different directions while trying to work his way to Dak. The battle is so loud from the clanking weapons and the screams of death. Dayne swings the releaser wildly sticking and stabbing anything she can. The Hangman grabs angels and rip their wings from their bodies. Dillo feels unstoppable in his new and improved shell. Colt never stops moving.

Hoss tackles the first Beast he comes to. The two giants exchange blows. Octoros climb all over the pair, making it hard for either to gain the upper hand. Hunter tries picking them off of Hoss with precise shots. Hoss, already covered in blood, bites and kicks like a wild horse trying to be ridden for the first time, throwing punches and spiders in all directions.

Dragons fly across the battlefield scorching the ground and any poor bastards in their paths. Demon dogs leap at any chance of grabbing a low flying dragon. Even with such an even battle, Dak's army pushes toward Paradise. Two Beasts reach the gates and pound on them. They're hitting the gates with such force that cracks begin to form in the walls. Kannon orders the knights to fall back and save the wall. Mav, Meg, and Russell lead the way. Reaching the first Beast, they run in different directions, slicing and dicing the legs of the Beast. Getting attention off the wall and on to them causes a few knights to lose their lights. Owl appears at the top of the gate with archers who fill the second Beast's face with as many arrows as it can hold, blinding the second Beast and making him stumble and fall into the gate, jarring it from the wall. With a big enough gap now between the gate and the wall, spiders and Shadows pour into Paradise.

Bug and Spin Doll stand back-to-back trying to protect one another. In mid swing, Bug catches a glimpse of Dak. He now has a new target.

Bug takes Spin Doll's hand and runs into the pile of corpses toward Dak. Bug rushes for Dak's blind side with his bat raised to strike. Footsteps away from reaching Dak, Bug is hit by a flying Octoro. This sends him soaring away from Spin Doll. Bug lands with such force, his vision blurs. Rubbing his eyes and trying to stand, Bug is trampled by a large demon dog. Now bloody and blurry, Bug tries to stand, but it's no use. He can't put pressure on his left leg. Being trampled must have broken it. Carcasses begin to pile up around him and soon engulf him.

Spin Doll frantically searches for Bug, but no luck; she's lost him. A well-timed blow to Hoss from one of the beasts sends a splatter of blood covering Spin Doll in a crimson color. Spin Doll wipes her face just in time to see a demon dog leap for her. With no time to avoid it, she stands her ground and holds her fan blades up. Both blades sink deep into the dog, as he bites into her shoulder. The dog tries to rip her arm off, as she loses all strength through the arm. She continues stabbing the dog with her strong arm, but she can't, for the life of her, get the dog to release its grip. Looking up, she notices Dillo on top of the dog. He's burying his dagger deep into the dog's skull repeatedly. Finally, Spin Doll feels the dog's pressure eases up. The dog collapses leaving a very tired Dillo and Spin Doll. Dillo has Spin Doll put her good arm over his shoulder, as he walks her out of the backside of the war. Once he thinks they're far enough out of harm's way, he sits Spin Doll on the ground to rest. She no longer has feeling in her left arm, and Dillo can see bite marks around her chest and back. Propping her up, he runs back into the battle to find Bug. Spin Doll feels this might be her last day as tears roll down her face.

Then… She can't believe her eyes—is she dreaming? Dillo comes from the battle, carrying Bug. He places a wounded almost lifeless Bug on the ground next to her. With her one good arm, she squeezes Bug tightly and keeps repeating to herself, "My husband, I need you to hold on. Hold on. I need you."

Bug has no movement. She watches his chest for any sign. It seems like forever, but his chest is slightly moving up and down. For the moment, her husband smiles and slowly moves his head onto her chest. Dillo stands nervously watching the couple, praying he isn't too late.

"Well, well, well, if it isn't Romeo and Juliet." The Hangman's voice comes from behind Dillo.

Dillo spins around shielding Bug and Spin Doll. He begins to stutter, "B-b-b-back away. I d-d-don't want to hurt you."

Hangman laughs at the idiot. "B-b-b-boy, get out of my way. These two will be trophies for my wall."

Suddenly a shadow covers Dillo and Hangman as Char lands beside her troubled friends.

"Hangman, leave now, or you'll be treated as you were before."

Hangman's eyes gleam. "Dragon! This will not be like our previous meeting. I assure you of that. This time you won't get to attack me from behind. It's been a long time since I released one of your kind, but I remember it like it was yesterday. Forty-two of your kind I have released and with any luck, I may reach fifty today!"

Char blows fire, engulfing Hangman in flames. Hangman, unfazed, continues to walk toward her. Char stops to take another breath. Now, still burning, Hangman gets close enough to grab her wing. Before she can fly away, Hangman makes a huge tear in her wing making her unable to fly. Octoros immediately climb all over her ripping and tearing her scales from her body. Frantically, she flails about trying to shake the spiders. But she can't remove them as they continue ripping her apart. After quite some time, Char lies there too exhausted to fight. The Octoros have done too much damage.

Hangman walks up to her and whispers in her ear and buries his fist deep into her chest, "You dragons think you're so powerful. But, like all the rest, you're just a big bird. Thanks for being forty-three." Pulling his hand from her chest, he holds up her heart like a trophy. Then he tosses it to the ground and stomps on it.

Dillo speechlessly watches the whole thing. His eyes roll in his head, as if he's thinking something. With Hangman's back turned toward him, Dillo runs up behind Hangman and hugs him. Hangman is caught off guard. He can't bend his arms enough to get Dillo off of him.

Dillo says, "I am so sorry for what you've been through. I love you, my friend."

Dillo continues to repeat the same words. Hangman has never felt love before. It's actually hurting him. Frantically, he tries reaching Dillo, but his arms just can't. Spin Doll watches in disbelief. Nothing can hurt Hangman. The more you attack and try to hurt him, the stronger he gets.

Dillo keeps repeating, "I am so sorry for what you've been through. I love you, my friend."

Hangman gets weaker with every 'I love you.' Dillo refuses to let the hug go as blood begins to trickle out of Hangman's eyes. It's as if he's crying blood. The two men fall to the ground, but still Dillo won't release the hug.

With his last breath, Hangman finally whispers, "Love hurts, but thank you, my friend." Slowly, Hangman begins to vanish.

Dillo, not letting go of his hug, leans up and kisses Hangman on his forehead. "Goodbye, my friend. May you no longer suffer in pain."

The Hangman is gone as he seeps into the ground. Dillo stands up with tear-filled eyes. "No one should die alone—no one."

Spin Doll can't believe the power of love is that strong. If everyone in this world and her last world had at least one friend who truly cares about them, there would be no need for the Horizon.

She softly says to Bug, "Why are so many people fueled by hate?"

Bug whispers back, "Love has been forgotten. When we need it most, no one will share."

Spin Doll hugs her husband as if she'll never let him go.

Chapter 51

"In a war so brutal, are there any winners or losers?" –Dillo

Hunter, exhausted, can hear Bob slapping everything near him. But his biggest surprise is watching Spazz handle his spear. He might be the first-person Hunter has seen that would give him a run for his money in a one-on-one battle. Knowing the beasts must be stopped, Hunter, Bob, and Spazz turn their attention to the closest one. Hunter fires round after round into the front of the Beast while Spazz stabs his spear into the right ankle of the it. With his power slap, Bob slaps the end of the spear clean through the Beast's ankle into the left one. This forces the Beast to fall to one knee. Thinking they have the Beast defeated, Spazz runs up to retrieve his spear. Hunter tries yelling to stop Spazz, but the noise from the battle makes it impossible for Spazz to hear him. Hunter sees the Beast notice the approaching Spazz. He begins firing even more to draw his attention. Spazz retrieves his spear and holds it up for Bob to see. Before any of them can react, the Beast grabs Spazz and bites him in half, spitting his upper half at Bob. Bob grabs both halves of Spazz and tries sticking them back together. Covered in his best friend's blood, Bob absolutely loses it. Spazz's body vanishes as his orb floats up to the stars. Hunter can only watch from a distance. Bob becomes so vicious, Hunter can't believe such a joking, loveable guy could become that angry.

Bob slaps the leg that holds the Beast up. The force of the slap brings the Beast to both knees. The Beast quickly grabs Bob, just like he had Spazz. Hunter fears the worst for Bob. But, unlike Spazz, Bob knows what's coming. When the Beast brings Bob close enough to bite him, Bob slaps him so hard that teeth fly from the Beast's mouth, sending him face down to the ground. Bob lands on his feet and slaps the Beast so hard and so many times the Beast's face caves in. Goo flies for half a mile as Bob continues to slap the Beast. With the Beast's life gone and sinking into the ground, Bob continues beating what's left.

Hunter must look away, which brings his attention to Hoss and another Beast's battle. He turns in time to see Hoss pile drive the Beast into the landscape, breaking the Beast's neck and back. Hoss sends the second one to the ground. A tired Hoss just lies there catching his breath, but he isn't too tired to give Hunter a thumbs up.

Meanwhile, Kannon finally works his way to Dayne. The two fight in total harmony with each other. It's an awesome sight to behold.

Dayne yells as loud as she can to Kannon, "I'm going back to Paradise! We must not let the gate fall."

Kannon nods while pushing forward. Dayne falls back and heads for the gate. Continuing to fight, she finds the gap between the wall and the gate. She glances in, only to see a dozen Shadows and a half dozen Octoros surrounding five of her knights. Knowing they're outnumbered, she squeezes through the crack and joins her knights. Mav and Meg are holding their own, but Russell and the other two have their backs against the wall. Dayne makes quick work of the Shadows with the releaser.

Saving the three knights, they move on to help Mav and Meg with the three Octoros. The Octoros seem much too large to fit in the crack Dayne used. She's more concerned with how they got in than releasing them. Mav slides under one of the spiders, exposing its abdomen. A quick upward thrust with his sword, and the spider disappears. Meg and Dayne make short work of another one. Once again, Russell and the other two knights find themselves backing up from the much larger Octoro. One of the knights stumbles, falling backwards. The Octoro releases him before he can regain his sword. Dayne and Mav act quickly and release the spider from behind.

With all the enemies from Paradise gone, filling the crack is the first priority. Mav and a few angels pile stone inside the crack, filling it enough to keep the enemies out for now. While mending the crack, the group pays no attention behind them. With a loud shriek, Dayne and the knights turn to see two demon dogs viciously shaking Russell and the other knight in their jaws.

"Where did they come from? The crack is filled."

"There must be another breach."

Trying to save the two knights is almost impossible without striking them, causing more damage. Russell draws his sword. Even with being shaken apart, he manages to get a fatal stab on his attacker. The dog falls and vanishes into the ground. Russ falls like a rag doll, unable to move. Knowing he's short for this world, he asks his queen to release his pain. Dayne never thought she'd have to release her own. But she gives him his wish and ends his pain. The other knight is released and lies dangling in the dog's mouth. All three warriors put the dog down at once.

Mav runs to find where these two could have come from. He soon notices that a wounded Beast is trying to throw the enemy over the wall. Mav focuses the remaining archers' attention toward the Beast. With hundreds of arrows piercing his body, the Beast is still trying to throw spiders over the wall. Hunter can see the angel archers struggling to bring down the Beast. Running at full speed, Hunter climbs the arrows in the Beast like stairs. Reaching the Beast's face, he quickly places two well-aimed shots into the eyes, blinding it. The stumbling Beast takes out as many of his men as he does theirs. Grabbing anything close to it and throwing it, the blind Beast fires two Octoros into the Paradise wall, making them splatter.

Dayne jumps down from the wall to join Hunter in releasing the Beast. The archers continue to fire arrows in the direction of the wounded Beast. By accident, one of the arrows pierces Hunter's right shoulder, dropping him to the ground. Seeing the arrow sticking out from his shoulder, Hunter quickly snaps it off and rejoins Dayne. Dayne slices and dices the Beast, trying to work him into position for Hunter to make the kill shot. Hunter will have to shoot the ends of each arrow simultaneously, driving them deep into its skull. Dayne finally has the Beast in position, but when she turns to let Hunter know he can take the shot, the Beast grabs her. He flings her back and forth, making Hunter's shot almost impossible. Hunter knows it's now or never, since

Dayne can't take much more of a beating. His friend is going to be released if he doesn't do something quick.

As Hunter raises his guns to take the shot, he realizes his right arm can't be lifted; the stray arrow makes it useless. He'll have to shoot bullets almost simultaneously with one gun. Without hesitation, he takes the first shot, followed by another less than a second apart. Just before the first bullet reaches its mark, the second bullet splits the first bullet, making both halves of the bullet hit its mark and driving each arrow into the Beast's brain. The force of the shot makes the Beast topple backward, taking out an Octoro. The Beast lands with no other motion.

Hunter quickly reaches a bloody and bruised Dayne, dragging her out of harm's way with his one good arm until Mav and Meg can help.

Once they get Dayne back behind Paradise walls, they call for Owl. He rushes up to the knights, not recognizing his queen.

"Owl, take care of your queen. She is not well."

"This is not my queen. This is a corpse," Owl states.

Hunter angrily insists, "You save your queen, or you'll join her."

Meg stays beside her queen as Hunter and Mav return to the war.

Chapter 52

"A much-needed day off can't come soon enough." –Kanon

Three days into the war, neither side looks as if they're winning. Dak looks more powerful than ever, and Kannon has the will to win. Something must give soon.

Seeing that his warriors are weak and wounded, Kannon orders everyone back behind Paradise wall. This way they can mend and regroup for a final push. Hoss helps the ones who can't make it back on their own.

Dak, realizing that they're seeking protection, orders his army to retreat as well. He must regroup and speak to his brother. The remaining dragons take their places perched on the wall.

After a few hours, all but Kannon are behind the gates. Hunter tries to persuade his friend to join them. But, from an agreement long ago, Kannon is never to step foot in Paradise. They do eventually talk Kannon into food and a wash, since he's so covered in blood, they can't tell if the blood is his or not. Kannon leans on the gates, listening through the patched crack.

Dak and his army of minions set up in sight of Paradise. With a long eye, Dak watches as his father never enters Paradise. He thinks the story must be true. His father made a deal with the stars. He gave up his right to Paradise and the sky in order for his wife to forever live there. If he enters the gates, then he'll sink into the ground never to return. So, his mother took her life in the last world. His dad made a deal with the stars to build him a door to the Horizon, just so he could make sure they kept the deal. When Kannon entered the Horizon through the door, the stars tricked him and smashed the door, trapping him there for eternity.

Dak mumbles, "More and more people came Here, giving up their lives. Father built the entire kingdom for those whom the stars wouldn't allow. They built the monster. He built the four towers in order to see his wife wherever she went in Paradise. Mother had the wall raised so she could see Father from wherever he stood. They would always be apart but remain together forever."

One of the Shadows overhears Dak talking to himself. "If they could never be together, how did you three become their children?"

Dak, now realizing that a lot of the army is listening to him, continues. "The stars tricked one other desperate man. The older gentleman made a similar deal, but it was slightly different. They told him that if he destroyed the kingdom and Paradise, they would give him Here. He agreed, but only if they placed Here between the two. Once the deal was finished, the old man and his wife would forever live Here. The old man had a silver tongue and was getting the two sides to agree to work with him and overthrow the stars. Once the stars heard of this, they approached the old man. But his wit and tongue tricked the stars into giving him a safe place in which nothing can harm him or his wife, not even the stars. The old man played everyone—the stars, the couple, and the Horizon. The stars were furious having been lied too twice. So, the stars made three children—Evil, Light, and Here. My father was given the Evil, but this child wanted nothing but to see death. So, my father buried him alive in a tomb of cement. Being that the child fed off death and had single-handedly eliminated the dragon race, his anger made him untouchable. Yet he lived in the tomb—trapped in his mind.

"My sister, with the voice of an angel, was given to my mother. She was pure of heart and loved everyone. When she was happier than normal, she would levitate off the ground and slowly spin with her arms out, spreading happiness. Then there was me. I was left in Here. Not given to my father or mother. It was as if I never existed. Sure, my mother made sure I had a roof over my head, but the love was never there. The old man saw this, and he approached me with a deal. He would trick my parents into believing they were simple like me. All I had to do was beg the stars for a meeting. After days of hearing me bitch to them, they agreed to a meeting. I told them to come as something innocent. If they intimidated me, I would not explain my plan to rid them all. At the meeting, the biggest star appeared in the form of a baby. While I explained to the child star my made-up plan, the old man snuck up behind the baby and ripped it from its protective bubble. Without its protection, the baby became ill. So ill, in fact, that the remaining stars fell as well. The child here had no choice but to agree to another deal. The new deal was that the stars would no longer decide what happens in the Horizon. No matter how a person arrived in the Horizon, once they did their time, they would become a star by the two leaders both agreeing on it."

The Shadow interrupts. "So the stars no longer have power?"

"My mother and father have the only say about the stars. Little did they know, I made a deal with the stars myself. If I can remove both of them, the Horizon is mine, and those who give up in their world will forever remain here under my control. Also, the stars get the right back to choose who becomes a star."

Another Shadow asks, "What about the old guy? If you don't remove him, he'll still control Here."

Dak wipes some blood from his face. "The old man? I offered to release him forever."

They all laugh as Dak mentions one last thing before catching some sleep. "My parents' deal was broken when the old man made the new one. So, my stupid father can now enter Paradise. But I doubt he'll take the chance. I've heard many tales like this but believe me when I tell them this is the truth. Tomorrow will end this war, and we'll stand victorious."

Chapter 53

"Not all family are friends, but good friends are family." –Kannon

Kannon listens intently through the crack as Owl goes over the situation.

Owl clears his throat while the battle-tired warrior assesses their wounds. "We can win this! Over half their army has been destroyed. Only two beasts are left standing."

Before he can continue, Mav barks back, "Only two left! Look at us—we're just a small percentage of what we started with. We lost our knights. Meg and I are all that's left. Our queen is barely hanging on—if she even will. Bug is broken, Hunter has the use of one arm, Spin Doll is only about fifty percent, and we've got the leader of evil standing outside the gate, hoping we help him regain his throne. I'm sorry, but if we're going out swinging, then let's do this, because I'm not sitting around waiting to be released."

"We do still have about twenty or so dragons." Owl points out.

Hunter nods. "Yeah, but we lost at least fifty of those baby dragons. If we let the remaining ones fight, it will surely be the end of dragons forever."

Hearing this, Kannon yells through the gate, "Warriors, send me a star cleaner! Send the other star cleaner to my wife. Now!"

IC flies over the gate and lands in Kannon's waiting hands.

"Kannon, you may talk to your wife," IC explains.

Kannon wastes no time. "Dayne! Dayne! Can you hear me?"

Dayne responds with a faint voice, "I hear you, my love. But the pain, I believe, may end our love."

"Hang on, baby, you're in Paradise. This is where you'll heal. I have no idea how to win this war, but if today is our last, know that I love you, and I will find you in the stars."

Dayne faintly answers, "If this is our last stand, then we'll go to the stars together. Wait for me, my darling. I won't be long."

IC then flies off southeast of the Paradise wall, leaving Kannon with wide-opened hands. Suddenly, the gates begin to rumble, opening slowly.

Kannon shields his eyes from the bright light. Once the gate is fully opened, the light reveals a silhouette of eight figures. When Kannon's eyes adjust, sees the group that's left. Meg and Mav each stand on an end. Spin Doll helps hold up a really beaten Bug. Hunter stands, holding his pool stick in one hand while the other arm dangles almost lifelessly. Owl worriedly stands beside a propped-up Dayne, while Mim sits upon her shoulder.

Kannon rushes to Dayne and picks her up, kissing her. He whispers, "I love you forever."

She whispers, "Forever."

Now standing in front of Paradise, the gates begin to close, shutting the warriors out.

"Why close the gates?"

Hunter, without looking at him, replies, "No one gets past the gate without the Queen's approval. I mean no one."

Hunter grasps his pool stick even tighter. Hoss, who was resting against the Paradise wall, stands to his feet and picks up a waiting Dillo off the top of the wall. Placing Dillo beside Meg, they all face Dak's forces. Distracted by Mim whispering in Dayne's ear, they all try to continue staring off at the still impressive army Dak controls.

Kannon tells Hoss to send the remaining dragon's home. Hoss, not sure why, does as he's ordered. And they watch the dragons fly off into the Horizon.

"Why would you send them away? Now we stand even less of a chance to survive." Owl questions.

Kannon looks down at Owl. "I will not be the reason for the dragons' demise."

Hunter looks up to the stars as he mumbles, "I've always wanted to be a star."

Bug smiles upon hearing this, which prompts him to say, "Looks like the final inning. Time to nut up or shut up."

Spin Doll, trying to lighten the mood, asks, "What about the ones who don't have nuts?"

Bug smiles. "You married me. You must be nuts." This brings a small chuckle to everyone.

Kannon steps out from the group and turns to face them. He clears his throat. "I am not a man who has friends, but yet here you all stand. Since I don't have friends, I consider you all family. I cannot stand here and watch my family die. You've all proven how important your stories are to me. Sure, your stories didn't evolve as you planned, but when you arrived here in the Horizon, you all became the authors of your own story. You rewrote your story. Only now it's up to me to make sure it ends happily. If this is our last fight, I hope we all meet again in the sky. This war was because of Dayne and I. I'm sorry you all were caught up in it. Love makes you do stupid things. When we arrived here, I made a deal with the stars to let us live here forever. They agreed, only to trick me into never being able to be with her again. We were placed on different paths, only to see each other from afar. We knew that if we disobeyed the deal, consequences would come for us. I'm sorry that you all must pay for our love. I didn't mean for you all to get hurt. Since this was caused by our selflessness, she and I will be the only ones continuing this war. You all may leave and hopefully continue writing your stories. Thank you."

Dayne steps forward, taking Kannon's hand. The group stands silent with their mouths gaping open as Kannon and Dayne begin to walk away.

After about ten steps, Bug's voice bellows out, "Fuck that! We're a family. We came into this world together; we'll leave it together. Besides, what kind of a watcher would I be if I didn't have my warrior's back?"

Kannon and Dayne smile without turning around, as the rest of the group joins in agreeing with Bug. Before any of them can take another step, the Paradise gate flies open. There in the opening stands Bob with a pile of sandwiches.

"Let's eat first. I don't know about you guys, but I can't whip ass on an empty stomach."

Everyone bursts out laughing as they join Bob and his pile of sandwiches.

Chapter 54

"When you have the upper hand, avoid hitting yourself." –Dak

Anger fills Dak once again as he hears laughter coming from his enemies. Perplexed, he cannot believe his ears. His enemies are truly laughing and joking.

He calls for his army to stand. With his fist in the air, he orders, "They are few. We are many. Let this battle end today. With no dragons remaining, and only a handful of them, attack the big one. Once he's released, it's over. Whatever you do, save my dad for me. Attack!"

The army charges toward the Paradise wall. Soon they have the warriors surrounded. Dak, even more fired up, watches the warriors feast on sandwiches and act as if his army doesn't exist. With only about twenty yards between the two sides, Dak demands, "Stop laughing, you idiots. Today is your last day in the Horizon."

Hunter yells back, "Shut up, boy! The men are talking."

Dak absolutely loses his shit from hearing this. "I will release you last, Hunter, so you can watch them all die. Now, who wants to be first?"

Kannon turns toward his son. "Boy, you talk as if you've won this war already. Sure, there's only eleven of us and a thousand of you, but we're a family. A family's love will conquer all."

Fuming, Dak yells back, "The only family here is you, me, mom, and Spin Doll."

"No, Son, you're wrong. Just because we're family does not mean we're friends. But really good friends become a family."

"Then, Dad, die with your family."

The army begins to slowly take steps toward the warriors as the warriors draw their weapons.

Suddenly, the ground begins to shake slightly. The evil army stops and begins looking toward the ground. Every few seconds the ground shakes and then stops.

Dayne's face draws a big smile as she softly states, "The Ones are coming."

Dak backs away to get a better look at who they are. With not too long a wait, Dak and the evil army begin to see something in the distance. The closer they get, the bigger they are. Dak has never seen such giants. Instantly, he orders his army to attack the approaching giants.

Dayne softly explains to her group, "When you treat your friends with truths and respect, they'll help you when needed."

"Man, am I glad they're on our side," Hoss adds.

Dak sends most of his army plus the two beasts toward the Ones, while he and a couple hundred attack the warriors.

Even with the numbers, Dak knows that the tide of the war is changing—and not in their favor. Trying to fight while watching his army being slaughtered like pigs, while off in the distance the smaller battle he can see spiders and dogs flying through the air. The Ones dismantle the beasts into pieces. Hearing the beasts scream and Octoros being torn apart is distracting Dak. His army is diminished in a matter of minutes. Knowing now that he is losing, Dak issues a challenge to Kannon.

The exhausted warriors and the evil army stop as Dak shouts, "Father! This can be over if you'd like to finish this man to man. Winner takes all. That way you'll not lose your friends' lights."

Kannon answers, "Just you versus me?"

Dak nods then calls back what remains of his army. He points to the ridge off in the distance. "I'll meet you up there. Come alone, or I'll have my army attack your family till none are left."

Kannon agrees as he ushers his tired men back to the gate. Dayne walks out to speak to the Ones' leader, while Kannon stands back and watches his wife talk to the giants. Dayne hands the giant something. The giant bends down on one knee as Dayne gives him a kiss on the side of his face. Standing back on his feet, the giants then walk off into the darkness as Dayne returns to the group.

Chapter 55

"Be careful not to waste a wish. We get so few of them." –Dayne

With both sides waiting for the final battle, Dak pulls his remaining best fighters around him. Once they finish the huddle and are in position to listen to Dak, he orders, "You two demon dogs—you go up on that hill and hide till I give you a signal to rip Kannon apart. The rest of you attack the remaining warriors and make them scream loudly so Kannon can hear their last words."

One of the Shadows questions, "Sir, there are only thirty or forty of us left. How will we defeat what hundreds of us couldn't?"

Dak slaps him in the back of his head as he answers, "You fool! You think I really thought what we brought would win this war? My second army should arrive within a couple of hours. My second round of Octoro babies should've hatched and be on their way to Paradise gates. If you imbeciles can survive long enough, you will see my power and watch as I take control of Paradise. Oh, to own all those priceless doors."

The evil huddle cheers as if they've already won.

* * *

On the other side, the eleven warriors sit in a circle, beaten and bruised. Kannon looks around the circle at all his friends. They gave him and Dayne everything they had. He stands up out of respect and approaches each separately, beginning with Hunter. Shaking Hunter's hand, he says, "Hunter, my friend, how do I thank you?"

Hunter smiles through his crimson stains. "My friend, if I could give you a moment with your love, I would go through this a thousand times." Hunter bows his head to rest as Kannon moves on to Dillo.

"Dillo, my friend, this isn't your fight. Go inside those gates and feed the ducks." Kannon rubs Dillo's head.

Dillo giggles and mumbles, "Ah, those ducks can feed themselves."

Bob is next. Kannon reaches down to shake hands, but Bob stands and bearhugs him. "Man! Just taking the battlefield with you is an honor. I look forward to finishing this and having one hell of a beach party."

Releasing the hug, Kannon turns toward Hoss. "My friend—my big, big friend. Oh, how I missed you. Even if you weren't so big, you'd still have the biggest heart out of all of us."

Hoss nods. "Sir, teach your son to respect the higher rank. Oh yeah! You got the first round of Starletta's after this." Both men chuckle.

Megan, Owl, and Mav are next. Kannon says, "You three! I owe you three more than you'll ever know for protecting my wife when I couldn't. If I'd had three protectors like you, we probably wouldn't be in this situation. Thank you."

All three hold their right hands to their foreheads and cover their hearts in a show of respect.

Spin Doll stands and hugs Kannon, but Bug can't make it to his feet. Kannon hugs Spin Doll in return. "Oh, beautiful Spin Doll. Your beauty is only beaten by your loyalty. Take care of my best friend. He truly knows you are his whole world. Be strong, my daughter, like your mother."

Spin Doll kisses Kannon's cheek and returns to Bug. Next, Kannon bends down and places both hands-on Bug's shoulders. Bug can barely lift his head to look at his friend. Kannon knows his friend is not in good shape, as he thanks him. "Bug, my best friend, I couldn't have gotten this far without having the best watcher in the Horizon. From here on out, I got this. Please go back to Paradise and live a happy life with your beautiful wife. If you had a wedding, I would have been tickled pink to be your best man."

Bug speaks slowly and softly, as if he doesn't have the strength to talk. "I like the sound of best friend. I'm sorry, my friend, I didn't mean to... Did you know Hunter was gay?"

Kannon replies, "Yes, I knew."

Bug exhales. "Really, I was the only one who didn't know." Bug begins to cry, knowing his friends are in a battle for their lives and he can't help.

Dayne is last, and she and Kannon wrap their arms around each other and then embrace in a kiss. The warriors watch, as though it will never end.

Kannon confesses, "My love, I lost you in our last life. I damn sure won't lose you in this one."

Dayne sadly replies, "When I got here, you were nowhere to be found. Then when you found me, I was shocked. With the Shadows playing so many tricks on me, I couldn't believe my own eyes. But when I found you at the cabin, my heart became yours again. Please don't go up on that hill. You know it's a trap."

Kannon, knowing he can't trust Dak, explains to Dayne, "I must. It may be the only chance we have left to save the Horizon and our friends. When I leave, take everyone into Paradise and lock the gates. You know it's not safe. His army will attack you as soon as I'm out of sight."

Dayne reassures him, "I'll get Bug to safety, but as for the rest of Dak's army, they must be released."

Before Kannon leaves, Dayne kisses him one last time. Hunter and a very weakened Bug stand. The three join in a hug. Kannon whispers, "I love you guys."

Hunter repeats him, "I love you guys."

Bug replies, "I love you guys, but not the way you think, Hunter."

All three of them laugh as they break the circle. Kannon walks away with the sound of Bug joking with Hunter. "Hunter, did you touch my ass? Because I'm pretty sure my ass got touched during that hug. For the last time—no means no!" Everyone laughs as Kannon walks away shaking his head.

Chapter 56

"Time, we finish what we started. Game on." –Dak

Dak reaches the top of the hill first, making the two demon dogs hide in the hedgerow out of sight. But he orders, "When I scream 'attack', you attack. Be ready to go for his arms. We need to disable his cannon." The dogs understand and go to their hiding spot.

Not long after that, Kannon appears from a small, wooded area. Dak speaks first. "Ahh, I thought maybe you wouldn't show, Dad. I mean, last time we tried this, I believe I was about to win before that Beast showed up and almost decapitated you."

Kannon scowls. "I don't believe that's how it went. I believe I was about to win. Maybe, just maybe, you called the Beast to save you. But you had me for a while, because, for the life of me, I couldn't figure out why you were untouched by the Beast. I guess that question is answered. So, what are you going to do without your Beast?"

Off in the distance, Kannon and Dak hear the sounds of swords meeting one another. Dak smiles. "Evil armies just don't listen like they used to. Oh well, at least your friends can join you."

Dak and Kannon draw their swords as Kannon powers up his arm. They begin to circle as Kannon questions, "Why would you want to release your mother? She's the only one who truly loved you."

Dak scoffs at that. "Loved me—did you say loved me? No, she cared for me. She loved you! Day in and day out, all I heard was how great a man you were. Well, I'm sorry I must prove her wrong. Sorry, Dad, but it's time for you to leave." Dak lunges at his father to no avail, as Kannon just sidesteps Dak's attempt. The two continue throwing shots that the other blocks.

Down by the Paradise wall, Bug is placed sitting against the wall with his bat in his hand. With not enough strength to lift it, it's more for show. The rest of the group pushes on, releasing everyone that tries to come for Hunter, who is deadly, even with only one arm. Spin Doll and Dayne run through the enemies like a hot knife through butter. Any of the larger Octoros and dogs are quickly dispersed by well-timed stomps from Hoss. Bob throws haymakers from way in the back that readily knock the souls from the spiders' bodies. Meg, Owl, and Mav have guard duty, guarding Bug. They're like a wall themselves. The army is evaporating with every swing of the warriors.

Back on the hill, Dak and Kannon seem to be at a stalemate. Neither can seem to gain the upper hand, with both totally equal at the moment and getting more exhausted with each swing.

Dak yells, "Attack!"

Two large demon dogs emerge from the hedgerow. They attack Kannon, knocking him to the ground. One of the dogs firmly locks its jaws onto Kannon's cannon and shakes its head viciously, trying to rip it from his body. The other dog stands firmly on top of Kannon, waiting for his turn.

Without any notice, the dog that's waiting is torn in half as blue goo splatters everywhere, followed by the dog ripping Kannon's arm explodes next. Kannon lies on the ground covered in goo. His arm is in really bad shape, as it spews red blood. The red blood mixes with the blue goo, making the battlefield purple. Dak covers his eyes to avoid the exploding dogs. When he opens them, they reveal a standing, injured Kannon and a fresh-looking Colt.

Kannon asks Colt, "Did you finish your task?"

Colt nods her head.

Kannon orders her, "Now go help the others!"

Colt nods once again and is gone.

Dak barks, "Your girl just ran through my dogs. What a sick bitch."

Kannon, struggling to stand from loss of blood, brags, "That other army you thought you had all has been released. They're not coming to save your ass. That little girl just made sure of that."

"I don't need them anyway! Once I end you, I'm king." Dak attacks his father with a flurry of swings, knocking Kannon to the ground.

Colt shows up in time to help finish the rest of the evil army. While they watch the last one fall, Spin Doll lets out a shriek. Bug is not where she left him. The ground and wall is covered in blue goo. Tears fill her eyes as they watch a light orb float to the sky.

Dayne quickly hugs her. "He was a warrior who loved you with all his heart. The warriors have won but lost a great friend."

Kannon tries getting back to his feet, but losing as much blood as he has, it's no use. With his father's back on the ground, Dak stands on top of him, gloating. He places one foot on his father's cannon and one foot on the other side of his body.

Standing directly over Kannon, Dak says, "You don't know how long I've waited for this moment. This is true power. Don't worry, Dad, I won't let Mom suffer much. Sis will make the perfect pet. Maybe I'll even get her a golden cage. The remaining warriors will be dismembered one limb at a time in Paradise's town square. Also, this will no longer be called the Horizon. I'm thinking of something like Dak Nation."

Kannon closes his eyes, trying to picture his beautiful wife. Dak is done talking and raises his sword above his head with both hands. His eyes grow large, but before plunging his sword deep into his father's chest, he adds, "Now my legacy begins!"

Kannon squeezes his eyes, bracing for the pain. He can feel the swoosh and hears the crack of a bat, but he feels nothing. He thinks to himself, *Am I dead?*

Then he hears, "That dog won't hunt!"

Kannon cracks his eyes open to see an outline of Bug reaching down to help him up.

Epilogue

"Even a bad day in this world is a good day. They're no guarantee what the Horizon will offer you." –Jim

Jim leans back on his bench, kind of happy now that his story has ended. Reaching into his pocket, he retrieves his friend from the dungeon cell and gently places the cricket on the bench. They sit for a bit, looking over the Horizon. Jim begins the conversation as if the cricket asked him a question. "You really want to know what happened to Kannon, Dayne, and the rest of them? Well, sit back, my friend, and I'll fill you in.

"After Bug knocked Dak out and saved Kannon, they placed Dak into the pit hole in the newly built barn. There he'll wait out his remaining days. The dragons returned to the cliffs in the sky, where they flourished. Did anyone ever tell you how they had so many for the great war? No? Well, when Bug exploded in the great kingdom battle, he not only changed all the Shadows solid, but he also unearthed many dragon eggs that were hidden many years ago by the last remaining dragons. Dillo was given the old couple's farm that he helped work on. Matter of fact, it's the largest farm in the Horizon—minus the geese, of course. It's called Papa's Dream, and right in the middle of it sits a giant stone turtle shell. Bob invited Hoss to hang at his beach, which is now called Bob and Hoss's Beach. They just drink Starletta's and work on their all over tans.

"Fat Jack's cave has been demolished, and now a beautiful park resides in its place. Both factory and barn, as I stated earlier, have been fully restored. The factory is now producing large numbers of Starletta's. The king's hidden oasis is now an Airbnb.

"Mim and IC have made sure all the stars were put back in their proper spots and cleaned, of course. They watch over Baby Bee, taking weekends off to visit friends.

"The kingdom looks better than it ever has. On the front gates, there's an etching of the Jokers, which reads above them 'No Clowns Allowed.' Lord Hunter has really turned it into a more respectable place, where everyone is welcome. Well, everyone but clowns. Sheriff Colt was given the duty of patrolling all the Horizon. If she spots any evil or Shadows, she and her team dispense of them quickly. She recruited Mav, Meg, and Owl as her erasers. High on the hill, where their first battle with the Beast took place, stand two large statues of Lakin and Cam. This is weird because some people claim they can't see Cam's statue during certain times of the day.

"Bug and Spin Doll moved into Dayne's little house. They had a set of twins—one boy named Hunton and a girl named Daylynn. They make sure the house is full of love, and visits to Grandma and Grandpa are frequent. Also, food fights are mandatory when Uncle Hunter is visiting, and so are pony rides from Aunt Colt."

Jim's friend begins to chirp, surprising him a bit. Jim laughs. "Oh! You want to know what happened to Kannon and Dayne, do you? Well, Kannon finally got the balls to step inside Paradise, and you know what happened? Nothing. Nothing happened. The evil star had lied to them. Finally, Kannon and Dayne were together again. They made the most of it because they had a lot of missed time to make up. Every night you can find them under the night stars, slow dancing on top of the Paradise wall."

The cricket brushes Jim's leg, as if to ask him how he's doing. Jim smiles at his friend and then answers, "I'm doing alright, I guess. The stars banished the evil star from the sky. The story goes that he was attacked by the last two remaining Octoros, and the three were dragged into the ground by a lone hand. As far as my Maggie, I will find her someday. I have to."

Jim bows his head down as tears begin to appear. He covers his face with his hands to help hide the tears from his friend. The cricket begins to rub his back legs together, playing one of the most beautiful songs Jim has ever heard. When the cricket finishes the song, it hops to the ground and leaves Jim sitting alone. Jim whispers, "Goodbye, old friend. Thanks for listening."

Jim leans back on the bench, now covering his face with both arms to hide his tears.

"Why are you so sad, James?" Maggie's voice asks.

Jim removes his arms to see his beautiful wife sitting beside him. He embraces her as if he'll never let her go again and mutters, "They're not tears of sadness, dear. They're tears of happiness."

They sit on the bench and watch the sunset, making the Horizon a beautiful shade of purple.

Jim whispers, "I love you, my Maggie."

Maggie softly replies, "I love you, my James."

Then they both whisper, "Forever," as the sun vanishes.

Days Not Wanted

When the day comes, and I'm no longer there,

It's nobody's fault; life just isn't fair.

My story was short. No one wants to hear.

I'll only miss out on my unwanted years.

This world was so hard. I couldn't find my place.

I'm sure no one will remember my invisible face.

This mean world may never hear all of my screams,

Because they are trapped inside of my dreams.

My pain is so real, and so are my fears.

I can't see any love from behind blurred tears.

This isn't the end.

I'm not saying goodbye.

I'm sure that you'll find me waiting on the other side.

Dear Readers:

If you enjoyed *Hidden In The Horizon*, I would be so grateful if you would consider leaving a review on Goodreads, Amazon, or Barnes & Noble (if you purchased it there). Reviews truly make a difference and help other readers discover the story.

Thank you from the bottom of my heart for taking this journey with me.

And if you haven't already, be sure to pick up the first book in the series, *Caught In The Horizon* — the story begins there.

www.ingramcontent.com/pod-product-compliance
Lightning Source LLC
Chambersburg PA
CBHW070221180726
47999CB00016B/211